BOOKS BY RUSSELL GINNS

SAMANTHA SPINNER

SPINNER

AND THE

PERPLEXING PANTS

SAMANTHA SPINNER

AND THE

PERPLEXING PANTS

RUSSELL GINNS

ILLUSTRATED BY BARBARA FISINGER

DELACORTE PRESS

Text copyright © 2021 by Russell Ginns
Jacket and interior illustrations copyright © 2021 by Barbara Fisinger
Image Credits: pp. 2, 144 (top right), 145, 240, 292: Shutterstock; pp. 144 (top left, bottom), 167: Pixabay; p.1: Horne, Andrew, 11 May 2010, "A photo of *The Thinker* by Rodin located at the Musée Rodin in Paris," digital image, Wikimedia Commons, web, 17 July 2020.

Visit us on the Web! rhcbooks.com

Educators and librarians, for a variety of teaching tools, visit us at RHTeachersLibrarians.com

Library of Congress Cataloging-in-Publication Data
Names: Ginns, Russell, author. | Skorjanc, Barbara Fisinger, illustrator.
Title: Samantha Spinner and the perplexing pants / Russell Ginns ; illustrated by Barbara Fisinger.
Description: First edition. | New York : Delacorte Press, [2021] | Series: Samantha Spinner series ; 4 | Audience: Ages 8+. | Audience: Grades 4–6. | Summary: It is up to Samantha and her brother Nipper to face what the WEATHER has in store for them and defeat SNOW, or risk losing their Uncle Paul forever.
Identifiers: LCCN 2020013072 (print) | LCCN 2020013073 (ebook) | ISBN 978-1-9848-4923-6 (hardcover) | ISBN 978-1-9848-4924-3 (library binding) | ISBN 978-1-9848-4925-0 (epub)
Subjects: CYAC: Adventure and adventurers—Fiction. | Brothers and sisters—Fiction. | Missing persons—Fiction. | Uncles—Fiction. | Family life—Fiction. | Mystery and detective stories.
Classification: LCC PZ7.G438943 Saf 2021 (print) | LCC PZ7.G438943 (ebook) | DDC [Fic] —dc23

The text of this book is set in 13.7-point Galena.

Printed in the United States of America
10 9 8 7 6 5 4 3 2 1
First Edition

TO SHELDON GINNS AND MARIAN COHEN

Thanks for encouraging my love of art,
architecture, and exploring the world.

The Thinker

A bronze statue of a man sitting on a rock with his chin resting in one hand is known around the world as *The Thinker*.

French sculptor August Rodin created his original plaster model in 1881, and he made dozens of bronze versions in many sizes over the rest of his career. The largest ones are more than six feet tall.

Like Leonardo da Vinci's *Mona Lisa* and Michelangelo's *David*, Rodin's *The Thinker* is one of the world's most famous works of art. Pictures of the sculpture are often used to represent ideas, inventions, and learning.

Today, twenty-eight giant bronze *Thinker*s sit in deep thought on steps of museums, in university courtyards, and at the entrances to buildings and parks in cities around the world.

The twenty-eight largest *Thinkers* sit atop entrances to super-secret tunnels around the world.

When you are at the Detroit Institute of Art, take a closer look at the stone base beneath the statue. Find the side that faces the museum. Grab a corner and pull. The heavy panel will swing outward and reveal a staircase.

The steps are covered with fine dust and can be slippery, so be sure to use the handrail as you enter.

Also, watch out for the SNOW!

CHAPTER ONE

THE BAD NEWS BLARES

"One hundred forty-four! One hundred forty-four!"

Sitting on the steps to his uncle's apartment over the garage, Nipper had thought he was far enough away from Sammy the parrot to not hear it screeching.

"The Yankees are the worst! One hundred forty-four!"

He wasn't.

Somewhere behind his neighbor's house, Missy Snoddgrass's double-triple super-awful pet bird squawked and blabbed. Nipper's Yankees were in big trouble, and the parrot made sure he knew it.

"Did you hear that?" said Mr. Spinner. "One hundred forty-four."

Nipper turned to see his dad. He stood a few feet

away, smiling, and waving a yellow-mitten-covered hand. In his other hand he was holding up a fresh, steaming waffle with a pair of tongs.

"That's a gross, Son," said Mr. Spinner. "Remember?"

"Yeah, Dad. I remember," said Nipper. "A dozen dozens is one gross. That rotten bird is squawking about a gross of games."

Ever since Missy had stolen his baseball team, the Yankees had been on an endless losing streak. It was a major-league catastrophe.

"Cheer up, Son," said his dad, waving the waffle tongs in front of him. "I've made you breakfast."

Nipper caught a whiff of the fresh waffle. It smelled delicious. The aroma was soothing. He would love a waffle. He would have one . . . maybe two . . . maybe three . . . waffles . . . three . . .

Nipper snapped out of it.

Three more games! His Yankees only had three games left!

He looked over to the Snoddgrass yard. He squinted and tried to spot Sammy the parrot. He kept looking, until his gaze fell on the back of the Snoddgrass house.

Nipper watched a green dot flickering on the covered porch.

"Come back inside with me," said Mr. Spinner. "When waffles get cold, the flavor decreases."

Nipper turned back to face his dad. In the four months since Mr. Spinner had taken over as the family's official breakfast maker, he had become a breakfast perfectionist. Nipper's dad applied science and math to waffle making. Normally that was awesome. But today it was just a distraction.

"I'll be there in a minute," Nipper said.

He watched his father walk back across the pavement and disappear into the kitchen. Then he looked again toward his neighbor's house.

"A gross of games," he repeated.

Nipper felt like *he* was caught in a *gross game*.

The New York Yankees had just lost their one hundred forty-fourth game in a row. If they lost three more times, they'd be finished. Gone. No more. According to rule thirteen hundred thirteen, section thirteen, any baseball team that loses one hundred forty-seven games in a season gets kicked out of the league. Their bats are chopped into firewood, and their uniforms donated to community musical theater groups.

He couldn't let it happen. Not musical theater. Not his Yankees. His precious, super-awesome Yankees!

Nipper eyed the paper bag in his hand. He had been carrying it with him ever since he and his sister had escaped from the Clandestine League of Unstoppable Daredevils, a band of skateboarders, surfers, and gymnasts also known as the CLOUD. He uncurled the top and peeked inside.

Good. The special thing inside the bag was still there. He was going to need it . . . if he was going to save his team.

CHAPTER TWO

MORNING, WARMING . . . WARNING!

Samantha's eyes snapped open.

"Where's Uncle Paul?" she shouted.

She looked around. She was in her room, alone.

She sniffed.

The scent of fresh-baked waffles filled the air.

Had Uncle Paul made breakfast?

No. It was her father downstairs in the kitchen. Of course it wasn't her uncle.

Uncle Paul was missing . . . again.

A little over a week ago, Samantha had found her uncle. She'd had to defeat ninjas, clowns, and daredevils to do it. Then, when she hadn't been around—the moment she'd turned her back—Uncle Paul had gotten taken . . . again!

It was Nipper's fault, and her father's fault, too.

She'd literally just gone upstairs, and a bunch of men and women in white coats and bright white sneakers had showed up at the house . . . and Nipper and her father had let them take her uncle away.

Again!

Nipper had said they were the "math police." But Uncle Paul had left behind an old, worn mitten and a note that said *Watch out for the SNOW!*

Samantha didn't know much more than that. The only thing she had learned from what had happened was that her brother and her father weren't much help at all, especially when it came to not losing Uncle Paul.

She sat up in bed and wiped sweat from her forehead.

Why was it so hot in the house?

She took in her surroundings. Her red umbrella rested against the side of her desk. She hadn't touched it for a week, not since her embarrassing fainting spell.

Samantha had blacked out right after Uncle Paul had been taken away. The doctor said it was due to travel stress, plus a severe attack of *coulrophobia,* a fear of clowns.

Samantha thought *that* was a bunch of hooey. She loved to travel. She had also defeated a band of awful clowns known as the Society of Universal Nonsense. That proved beyond the shadow of a doubt that she wasn't afraid of clowns.

Samantha's mother said her blackout could also have been caused by the shock of seeing Buffy in a photo with a cute new boyfriend. And it was true that Samantha had been shocked. Her sister was completely awful. It didn't make sense that the boy who had saved Samantha and Nipper in Africa had suddenly shown up in California. And it made even less sense that he was there with Buffy.

But what did her mother know about those things, anyway? Dr. Spinner *was* a doctor, but all her patients were rodents and lizards.

It didn't matter. Samantha had slept, rested, and thought about missing uncles, annoying brothers, unhelpful fathers, and ridiculous selfish older sisters for a solid week. It was time to make new plans. And time to find Uncle Paul once and for all.

But that was hard to do when it was so *hot* in the house.

She got up and went to the window. She pulled it open, and a cool, fresh, Seattle summertime breeze wafted into her room.

Much better.

Samantha saw her brother in the backyard, making his way to the house. They hadn't spoken much to each other in the past seven days. At first it was because Samantha had fainted and stayed in bed for a day and a half. Then it was because he wouldn't apologize for letting the people in white coats take Uncle Paul away.

"Watch out for the SNOW," she repeated now.

Was the SNOW the people who had taken her uncle away? Who could they be, and why had they done it?

She had spent enough time resting, and moping. It was time to figure things out. She got dressed and opened her bedroom door. A gust of warm air rolled in from the rest of the house.

Breakfast smelled delicious. And she was ready to talk to Nipper again, even without his apology. She would let him rattle on about his baseball team, and then they could start making plans to save their uncle from the SNOW.

CHAPTER THREE

WEATHER OR NOT

"Dad," Samantha called as she walked into the kitchen. "Why is it so hot in here?"

Her father stood at the counter, adjusting the controls of the waffle iron. He wore the yellow mitten from Uncle Paul on his right hand, and he held a pair of tongs in his left. A six-high stack of waffles rested on a plate nearby.

"And why aren't you using an oven mitt?" she added.

"All the oven mitts are missing," he answered. "It's a good thing Paul left us this mitten."

Dennis sat on the floor, close to the kitchen table. He looked wilted. His head drooped inside his plastic cone. The temperature was too much for the little pug.

"Why is it so hot in here?" she asked again.

"Your mother and I decided to turn up the heat," her father said as he poured batter onto the waffle iron. "The radio warned about a cold snap this afternoon."

"Cold snap?" asked Samantha. "Have you looked outside? It's warm and sunny."

"We also got a text alert about a blizzard coming," said Mr. Spinner.

"A text alert?" asked Samantha. "Who sent that?"

"It came from the Storm Notifications of Oregon and Washington," he answered.

"Storm Notification of . . . I've never heard of . . . ," said Samantha. "Wait! Did they call themselves the SNOW?"

"Possibly," said Mr. Spinner. "The alert sounded very serious."

He closed the waffle iron and stepped back from the counter. Then he took a handkerchief from his pocket and mopped his brow.

"But you're right," he said. "It's quite hot in here."

"Where's Mom?" asked Samantha.

"Your mother went to the store to pick up an ice scraper. Just in case," said Mr. Spinner. "She's stopping at her clinic on the way home. Half her patients are cold-blooded, you know."

"I know," said Samantha.

Nipper entered through the back door and stopped in his tracks.

"Whoa!" he said. "Why is it so incredibly hot in here?"

"Okay, you've convinced me," said Mr. Spinner, pulling off the mitten and handing it to Samantha. "Take over while I go turn off the heat."

Before she put it on, Samantha noticed that something was trickling out of the mitten. She let a little bit collect in her open palm. It looked and felt like sand, but it was white.

"Salt?" she asked.

"I prefer my waffles unsalted, thank you very much," Nipper said, sitting down at the table.

Samantha tossed the mitten onto the counter. Then she carried the plate full of fresh waffles to the table. Nipper watched eagerly, but she didn't set it down.

"I need your help finding Uncle Paul," she told him. "So I have a deal for you."

She waved the plate of waffles in front of his face.

"I'll give you all these waffles. Unsalted. Then we start making a plan to find Uncle Paul. Along the way, you can complain about the Yankees losing . . . for a whole five minutes."

Nipper bit his lip. He seemed to be considering it.

"Fifteen minutes?" he asked.

"Okay. Fifteen. That's the maximum time limit, though," said Samantha.

Nipper sniffed the air.

"Can I complain a bit about the waffle that's starting to burn over there, too?" he asked.

Samantha turned to see smoke billowing from the waffle iron on the counter. She dropped the plate in front of her brother and dashed to the counter. She picked up the mitten, put it on, and lifted the lid to the waffle iron. With her other hand, she used the tongs to save the waffle. It was still mostly golden brown.

"Yes, Nipper," she said. "It includes this— Ouch!"

The hot lid touched her hand through a hole in the faded yellow mitten. She loosened her grip on the tongs, and the waffle fell to the floor.

"Wruf!" barked Dennis, suddenly alert.

The Spinners' pug darted across the floor, grabbed the waffle, and disappeared through the doorway. Samantha heard his plastic cone rattling down the hall.

She set down the tongs, removed the mitten, and examined her hand.

The waffle iron lid wasn't hot enough to have burned her badly, but it had left a little red mark on the edge of her right palm, just below her thumb.

She carried the mitten over to Nipper and sat down next to him.

"See this hole?" she asked, pointing to a tiny circle below the thumb. "I think Uncle Paul made this on purpose."

Nipper looked at the mitten, too.

"Why would Uncle Paul leave a mitten in the kitchen, especially one with a hole in it?" asked Nipper.

He took a big forkful of waffle and chewed. He paused and looked thoughtful. He chewed some more.

Samantha didn't have an answer. Her uncle was mysterious, but he always did things for a reason.

"Shake a little more of that salt onto my waffles," said Nipper. "It tastes surprisingly good."

Samantha started to get annoyed, then stopped.

She looked at the red dot on her open hand again . . . and smiled.

"Finish your breakfast," she said. She dangled the mitten and shook it, sprinkling salt onto his waffles as she spoke.

"I'll go get my umbrella," she told him.

She turned off the waffle iron and unplugged it.

"And then we're going to find Uncle Paul . . ."

She held up her right hand, with the palm facing her brother.

". . . in Michigan," she finished.

"Why Michigan?" Nipper asked. "And how are we getting there? No more traveling in a ball. I'm done with that."

Samantha had already decided not to say much more before they reached their destination. She wanted to make sure this truce with Nipper would last.

She left her brother with his waffles and went to fetch her umbrella—her red umbrella with the super-secret plans on the inside. It was the special gift her uncle had left for her when he'd disappeared the first time—and the best, most important tool she had for finding him. By the time she came back, Nipper was just finishing his breakfast.

"Do you have your hand lens with you?" she asked.

He reached into his pocket and held up his magnifying glass.

"Almost always," he said through a mouthful of waffle.

"Good," she told her brother. "Let's go."

"Go?" asked Nipper, swallowing with a gulp. "Go to Michigan? Why?"

"Whoopsy," said Samantha. "Your fifteen minutes just started. Come on."

She folded the yellow mitten in half and slid it into her back pocket. Then she crossed to the back door, opened it, and walked out.

On the walk to downtown Seattle, Samantha heard all about the wonderful New York Yankees, the lousy Los Angeles Dodgers, the rotten Boston Red Sox, how Missy Snoddgrass had stolen his Yankees, and the three games that stood between the Yankees . . . and doom.

CHAPTER FOUR

ROLL OUT

"I knew it," said Nipper, looking up at the elephant-shaped neon sign. "You're putting me back into a ball."

"Well . . . yes," said Samantha. "But I'm going with you this time."

"You're putting *us* back into a ball," Nipper complained.

This was exactly why Samantha had decided not to tell Nipper exactly where they were headed.

A little more than a week ago, their very unpleasant neighbor, Missy Snoddgrass, had trapped Nipper inside a giant ball of yarn. He'd rolled away and ended up inside the *kogelbaan*, a huge, underground, person-sized marble machine. Monkeys and daredevils had chased him. A French detective had arrested him. A thief with rainbow hair had thrown metal boomerangs at him, too. Clearly it had been a rough experience. Every time her brother talked about it, the story grew more dramatic and dangerous, and took longer to tell.

Samantha was pretty sure her brother's complaining wasn't really about the *kogelbaan*. Nipper loved roller coasters. Sometimes he rode them until he barfed! He was actually just upset about the Yankees, and it was turning him into a major-league whiner about everything.

But the *kogelbaan* had definitely been an amazing discovery. And it was a super-secret way for them to travel to Michigan . . . and look for Uncle Paul.

Samantha spotted the hidden button on the side of the Elephant Car Wash.

"I'm doomed," Nipper said quietly, staring at his shoes. "Everyone is doomed."

"You have exceeded your maximum time limit for whining," said Samantha. "Besides, we're not riding this for long—we're just taking the ball to the next station."

He shook his head and seemed to snap out of it a little.

"Okay, Sam," he said. "I'm ready for this ball game."

"Good," she said. "Now stand back."

She reached out with her umbrella and tapped the button. A section of wall slid sideways. Water splashed around the entrance, but they stood far enough away to stay dry.

"Follow me," she told Nipper.

Samantha slung the umbrella over her shoulder and glanced at her hand. A few stray salt crystals sparkled on her palm. She was pretty sure it was Uncle Paul who had put salt into the mitten before he'd left with the SNOW. But why?

In a spray of mist, she began to slide forward on the slick tile floor. As if balanced on an invisible surfboard, Samantha put her hands out and coasted down the long, wet passageway.

"Foul balls," she heard Nipper mutter behind her as she slid into the secret underground lobby leading to the *kogelbaan* station.

CHAPTER FIVE

SEE SALT

When Nipper had gotten lost inside the *kogelbaan*, Samantha had had to recruit several friends and roll across the country to save him. She'd even had to defeat the CLOUD along the way.

It had been an amazing adventure, but the *kogelbaan* was an unpredictable and confusing way to travel. Samantha hadn't planned to explore the marble coaster again for a while—at least until after she'd saved Uncle Paul. And yet there they were, rolling under the United States, inside a giant sphere.

Ten minutes after they'd boarded their ball, they exited out of the *kogelbaan* station at Allen Park, Michigan. Above them, a colossal car tire rose into the sky.

"The hole in the mitten was right here," said Samantha.

She held out her open hand for her brother to see and pointed at the tiny red dot where she'd gotten burned.

"If my hand were a map of Michigan, this dot would be just outside Detroit. Allen Park is just outside of . . ."

Her brother wasn't looking at her hand. He was staring past her, over her shoulder.

"Whoa, Nelly!" said Nipper. "It's the world's biggest tire!"

Samantha had forgotten that this was new for Nipper. When he'd first stumbled into the *kogelbaan,* his trip had been a tumbling out-of-control ride. Nipper had rolled past this stop on the marble coaster. He'd been too out of control to take a closer look at things, even if he'd wanted to.

Samantha, on the other hand, had used a map and then changed course to reach this exact spot to help her brother find his way home.

"The Uniroyal Giant Tire is eighty-six feet high and weighs eleven tons," said Nipper.

But of course her brother knew all about it. He was a member of WRUF—the Worldwide Reciters of Useless Facts—and a colossal tire was exactly the kind of thing that a WRUF member would memorize and recite.

Samantha looked to her right. In the field close by, she knew they'd find a pit with monocycles—electric, one-wheeled vehicles. She and her friends had ridden them from here to Kansas. The SNOW, however, probably didn't know about the monocycles, and she doubted that her uncle would let them in on that super secret. If there were any clues about the SNOW, they had to be nearby.

"Let's look for any sign that Uncle Paul or the SNOW have been here," she said.

A busy, six-lane freeway ran along one side of the giant tire. Samantha decided they should head in the other direction. But she also didn't want her brother to get distracted by the monocycles. He had enough trouble keeping focused without seeing a cool new vehicle. She led him away from the freeway, steering clear of the monocycle pit, and continued across the field.

They reached a clearing at the edge of the field that Samantha hadn't noticed the last time she'd been in this location. A dirt path lead to a cluster of single-story, industrial-looking buildings.

Something sparkled. Samantha looked down and stopped. Nipper bumped into her.

"What gives, Sam?" he asked. "Did you find something?"

"Maybe," she answered.

Samantha knelt and ran her finger across the path. It felt sandy. She held it out for her brother to see.

"Salt?" he asked.

She nodded.

The sparkling grains continued along the trail and disappeared into a building.

"Let's go there," she said, pointing to the structure.

They followed the salt to a corrugated aluminum building with a sign stenciled over the door:

SALT NATIONAL OVERSTOCK WAREHOUSE

"The SNOW?" asked Nipper.

"Seems like it," said Samantha. "But I don't think that's what the acronym stands for."

She jiggled the door handle. It wasn't locked. She pushed, and the door creaked open. A small cloud of dust drifted out from the doorway. She coughed.

"I guess nobody's home," she said.

"Snowbuddy?" asked Nipper. "Did you just say 'snowbuddy's home'?"

"No, I didn't," said Samantha. "Come on. We have to find Uncle Paul."

"Have it your way, Sam," said Nipper. "I'm just trying to inject a little humor into this adventure."

Samantha didn't respond. She wanted to get busy saving her uncle. She didn't need anyone to inject any humor. She held the door open and waved for her brother to enter the building.

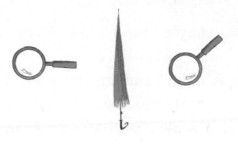

CHAPTER SIX

DUST THE TWO OF US

Samantha and Nipper stood, alone, in a strange store. Propped on a counter, a handwritten sign said:

BACK SOON
OUT BUYING SNOWSHOES

They were in a long room, lined with shelves and display stands filled with row upon row of boxes, bags, and other containers. Some of the containers were small, the size of a bag of flour. Others, resting on the floor, were as tall as Samantha, or even taller.

"Rock salt," she said, reading one of the boxes.

"Table salt," said Nipper, reading a large can.

On every shelf there was some type of salt.

Samantha coughed gently. The air was thick with salt dust.

"De-icer is nicer," said Nipper, reading a painted sign above a rack of saltshakers.

"Unfreezing is pleasing," replied Samantha as she read a carved salt plaque.

"Prints in the salt. I think it's a clue," said Nipper.

"Is that supposed to rhyme?" asked Samantha.

"No, Sam," he answered, pointing to the floor. "I think I found a real clue here on the floor."

Samantha looked down. Nipper was right. Dozens of footprints snaked along the salty floor. Most of the prints were from boots or sneakers. These soles were filled with patterns. One set of prints, however, left no pattern on the floor. They were just solid shapes.

Samantha and her brother both said it at the same time.

"Flip-flops."

Their uncle wore bright orange flip-flops all day, every day. Nipper actually had found a real clue. They were definitely on Uncle Paul's trail.

Nipper got down on his hands and knees and used his hand lens to study the footprints. As he moved about the floor, he stirred up a cloud of salty dust.

Samantha felt dirty, and sticky. She licked her lips and they tasted salty.

"When I get home, I'm going to spend an hour scrubbing off all this salt," she said.

She watched Nipper, crawling on the salty floor.

"You should, too," she told him.

"I can't really see that happening," said Nipper.

"Oh, come on," said Samantha. "Do you always have to be exceptionally gross?"

"No, Sam," Nipper replied. "These footprints lead over here, and they just stop. I really can't see how it's happening."

Samantha squinted at the trail of flip-flop prints. They led up to a wall and stopped. She followed the prints to the wall and took the umbrella from over her shoulder.

"Close your eyes," said Samantha.

"Why?" Nipper asked.

"It's about to get even saltier," she said, and she began to open and close the umbrella. It kicked up a breeze, sending salt flying everywhere.

Samantha closed her eyes and counted to ten, then stopped pumping the umbrella.

"Okay," she said. "You can open your eyes now."

Just as she'd hoped, the breeze had cleared most of the salt away from the wall, revealing the outline of a rectangle.

"A secret door?" asked Nipper.

Samantha nodded.

"Sometimes you have to take a closer look at things," she answered. "And clean up a bit, too."

She reached out and pressed the wall, and it swung forward. Beyond, a staircase led down into some kind of a cave.

"Let's go," she said to Nipper as she wiped her hand on her pants. She was definitely going to clean up when she got home. She had no idea how long from now that would be, though.

CHAPTER SEVEN

UNACCOMPANIED MINERS

Samantha and Nipper stopped at the bottom of the stairs. They stood at the entrance to a long, wide cavern. The walls sparkled. The huge space seemed to have been carved from salt.

"Whoa," said Nipper, pointing at the sides of the cavern with both index fingers. "We're in a treasure chest."

Samantha looked around. The walls of the chamber were lined with statues. People, animals, obelisks, and other shapes stood every few feet. Some of them looked like stone; others were glasslike. Some of the statues looked as though they had been painted with gold.

"It's Neptune again," said Nipper.

A statue of a large man and four horses stood in a

space close to one of the chamber walls. It looked just like the statue that Samantha and her brother had seen in Florence, Italy. Except that this one was only half as big, and it looked like it was made of glass, not white marble.

"Somebody copied the one in Florence," she told Nipper.

As she continued looking around, Samantha began to recognize a lot of the other statues. She saw a small version of the Statue of Liberty. It was white, not green. She also spotted a miniature arch, like the Gateway Arch in Saint Louis, Missouri. But this one was white, too, not silver.

"I think these things are made of salt," said Samantha. "Or some other kind of crystals. And I think everything here is a copy of something famous."

Here and there, baskets of gems rested on the ground. Nipper bent down and picked up a big blue gem.

"A diamond?" he asked. "Hope?"

Suddenly the gem crumbled between his fingers.

"Nope," said Samantha.

"This reminds me of that tomb in Egypt," said Nipper. "The one with all the treasures . . . And that big pit."

Samantha nodded. This cavern was like one big treasure room . . . of fake treasures. It looked like a long journey to the other end of the place. She waved her brother forward.

"Come on," she said. "Let's see where this goes."

"Hang on," said Nipper. "I'm thinking."

Nipper began moving his finger along a smooth section of cavern wall, drawing in the dust.

Samantha watched, realizing it was some sort of geometric shape.

A diamond.

He kept drawing, adding more shapes on the wall.

It was a *baseball* diamond.

Samantha whipped out her umbrella again. *Clang! Clang! Clang!* She banged the tip of her umbrella against a metal bin. The sound reverberated through the cavern.

"Maximum time limit exceeded!" she shouted, exasperated.

Nipper looked back at his sister.

"You have a one-track mind," Samantha continued.

"Fine, Sam," said Nipper. "But . . ."

"But what?" she pressed.

Nipper looked around, then back to her.

"But you're wrong," he said. "This isn't a one-track mine."

"Did you say *mind*?" Samantha asked. "Or did you say . . ."

"Mine," said Nipper. "As in 'Hey, Sam, you're banging your umbrella on a mine cart.' "

She took a closer look at the big metal bin. It was connected to a second bin, and each one had four wheels. The wheels rested on a track that ran into a wide tunnel.

Her brother was right. It was a little train.

"I call front," said Nipper as he climbed over the side of the little metal hopper. A cloud of salty dust rose when his shoes hit the bottom of the bin. Samantha pulled herself up and over the side of the rear cart. She tried to be more careful than her brother, but it didn't matter. White dust streaked her shirt and pants. That was just how it was going to be.

"All aboard?" asked Nipper.

She could see he had his hand on a lever that stuck out of the floor on the left side of the cart.

"Go for it," said Samantha.

Nipper smiled and shoved the lever forward.

Chugga-chugga-chugga-ga-ga . . .

A motor somewhere under their carts started to shake. The cart began moving forward. Slowly it picked up speed.

Samantha smiled. She had no idea where they were going, but super-secret travel was the way she was going to find Uncle Paul.

As she sped along in the cart behind her brother, Samantha watched his hair flapping in the breeze.

Nipper looked back at her. He took a deep breath, and his mood seemed to lighten a bit.

"Okay, Sam," he said. "I guess I have been moping about my Yankees a little too much."

Samantha nodded and watched the walls of the mine pass by.

They rolled on through the wide, dusty tunnel. Lights flashed as they passed beneath them. Every hundred feet or so, they rolled past a statue. Samantha recognized a full-sized copy of Michelangelo's *David,* and another statue that looked like George Washington. She saw Chinese warriors, horses and lions, and many other figures that didn't look familiar at all.

Samantha glanced at Nipper. He had his hand open and seemed to be staring at one of his fingers. In front of him, something had been rubbed into the dusty surface along the rim of the front panel of the mine cart.

"It would be great if you could keep yourself from touching everything for a while," said Samantha. "There's a layer of dust, dirt, and salt everywhere in this mine, and we both know you're not going to wash your hands anytime soon."

"I didn't touch anything, Sam," said Nipper. "I'm just looking at my ring finger."

In front of him, she could see there were letters scrawled on the dusty cart.

"Is that so?" she asked him. "Then who wrote those words on the cart right where you are—"

Samantha stopped herself. She squinted at the letters more closely. Six words appeared in the dust:

THE PATTERN IS IN THE PLAID

"Do you think Uncle Paul wrote this?" Nipper asked.

"I think so," said Samantha. "What could it possibly mean?"

"I haven't the foggiest idea," said Nipper.

"The pattern is in the plaid," she read.

At last, she had a clue . . . but she had no idea what it meant.

The tunnel had become broader. They rolled on, passing sculpture after sculpture.

Two more versions of Michelangelo's *David* went by, then a huge copy of the Lincoln Memorial. Between the sculptures, Samantha could see that there were many other lines of tracks leading to who knows where.

The cart began to slow.

"End of the line," Nipper called.

The cart bumped a metal post and came to a stop. They climbed out of the train and stepped into a narrow, dusty space.

Samantha looked back at the long, statue-lined tunnel. Now, at the end of the line, there was only one way to go. A metal staircase rose one flight to a small landing. Samantha and Nipper headed up the steps and stopped at the landing. There stood a door with three letters on it:

DIA

"DIA?" asked Nipper.

Samantha shrugged.

The door looked heavy, made of speckled stone. Maybe it was granite. A brass pole ran up and down along one side, forming a handle.

"The pattern is in the plaid," Samantha repeated.

"Come on, Sam. Help me with this," said Nipper, tugging on the door handle. It wouldn't budge.

She put her hands on the handle beside his. Together they pushed open the door.

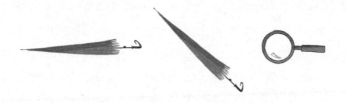

CHAPTER EIGHT

I DON'T THINK SNOW

Scra-a-a-a-pe!

The heavy door swung away from them. The Spinners stepped out into sunlight.

Samantha took a deep breath and let it out slowly. It was good to be out of the dusty mine and back in the fresh air. She shook herself off and stomped her feet to try to get rid of the dust.

She looked back. They had just emerged from the stone base of a huge statue. A man made of bronze towered above them. He sat on a rock, with his chin resting on one hand. The figure stared forward, as if he were deep in thought.

"*The Thinker,*" said Samantha.

Uncle Paul had told her about this sculpture many

times. It was by the French artist Rodin, and there were dozens of copies of it around the world. She pictured her uncle, imitating the sculpture as he sat on the steps to his apartment. She remembered how he'd had trouble keeping his chin on his fist as he spoke. Uncle Paul was the kind of storyteller who waved his hands in the air a lot.

"DIA," said Nipper, pointing up in the other direction.

Stretching out ahead of them, a wide staircase led up to a majestic building. Stone arches framed an entrance with ornate metal doors. Words carved into the stone above the arches read:

The Detroit Institute of Arts

"The DIA," said Nipper.

Samantha nodded at him. Then the two of them stood at the bottom of the steps and gazed up at the museum.

Several dozen people were lined up single file, waiting to enter the building. Samantha and Nipper joined them.

As she stood there, Samantha puzzled over the message from their uncle again.

"The pattern is in the plaid?" she asked Nipper.

He shrugged and turned to the line ahead of them.

He scrunched up his forehead. He began tapping his fingers on the sides of his legs.

Samantha knew that face and that tapping. He was getting impatient.

"Ugh," said Nipper. "I don't think this line's moving at all."

Samantha was used to hearing that from her brother also. From amusement parks, to movie theaters, to all-you-can-eat restaurants—any place you had to wait in line—Nipper complained that lines didn't move fast enough. And yet . . . this time he was right. The line to get into this museum was definitely not moving.

She looked back. A dozen people now stood in line behind them. She leaned out and looked up at the entrance again. A security guard stood blocking the doors. A sign beside him was taped to the top of an orange plastic cone. In handwritten letters, it said:

MUSEUM CLOSED DUE TO BAD WEATHER

She pointed to the sign and rolled her eyes.

"Bad weather?" asked Nipper, looking around. "It's a beautiful day."

"Exactly," she replied. "There isn't a cloud in the sky."

Nipper looked up.

"You're right, Sam," he said. "And why would an in-door museum close for bad weather anyway?"

Samantha looked back and forth at all the people in the line with her. They talked among themselves. They used their phones. None of them seemed to be taking a closer look at things.

"Come on," she said. "Let's investigate."

She stepped out of the line and waved for Nipper to join her. Then they marched up the stairs.

"Sorry, kids," said the guard as they reached the top. "We're not open."

In one white-gloved hand, the guard held a tally counter, a metal clicker to count visitors. His other hand was out, stopping the Spinners from touching the doors.

"There's been a blizzard today," he said. "A terrible ice storm. Hail the size of baseballs. Museum's closed."

"Really? Since when?" Nipper asked.

The guard scowled.

"Since we got all the alerts," he answered.

Samantha looked up at the sky, and then all around the steps of the museum. There wasn't any ice. There was no baseball-sized hail. It was a sunny summer's day.

"Who alerted you?" she asked.

"We got a phone call and a dozen messages from the SNOM," said the guard. "The Storm Network of Ohio and Michigan. Half our museum staff is out buying shovels and de-icer."

"Waitaminute," said Samantha, trying to sound calm and helpful. "Do you *see* any ice or snow?"

The guard looked around the steps.

"Nah," he replied.

"Do you *feel* any cold air?"

"No . . . ," said the guard carefully.

"Maybe this was a test," she said.

"A test?" asked the guard.

"Yeah," said Samantha. "The museum could be testing you to see if you have what it takes. You know, the power of observation. Maybe they want to invite you to join STARCH."

"STARCH?" asked the guard.

"The Stolen Treasures and Artwork Recovery Convention and Hoedown," said Samantha.

The guard nodded, just a little. He seemed to be thinking this over.

"Okay," he said. "I guess you can go in."

He smiled and clicked his tally counter twice.

"*Next* time, you should take a closer look at things," said Nipper.

"What?" the guard asked. He stopped smiling.

"STARCH doesn't like it when their members stand around blocking doors," Nipper said.

The guard began to look irritated.

"They have a lot of great snacks and cookies at STARCH parties, and they might not want you to—"

"Don't annoy him," Samantha whispered, tugging Nipper's shoulder. "He's letting us in."

She pulled her brother through the doors of the museum.

As they walked through a foyer and into the main lobby, Samantha marveled at Nipper's special talent for annoying people in mere seconds.

CHAPTER NINE

ARMORED AND DANGEROUS

Samantha and her brother walked to the center of the museum's lobby and gazed up a grand marble staircase leading to a grand hallway.

"Let's head to the landing up there and have a look around," she said, using her umbrella to point up to the second floor. "It's as good a place as any to get started."

They climbed the steps to the top, where a broad hallway stretched out ahead of them. On each side, doorways led to the museum galleries, and far ahead there was a huge two-story entrance to somewhere beyond.

"Good night!" said Nipper.

"What?" Samantha asked.

Samantha glanced around to see what her brother was talking about.

"I meant *knights*," he said. "You know, with a K."

He smiled at her and pointed sideways.

Between the entrances, tall glass cases lined the hall. Inside each one, a shiny silver knight stood at attention. They weren't actually people. They were empty suits of armor. A knight who wore one would be covered from head to toe in metal. A few small slits would have let the wearer see and breathe, but that was it.

"I wonder what these guys did when they had to go to the bathroom," said Nipper.

Samantha smiled. Normally her brother's comments were ridiculous. But she had been wondering the same thing.

"I guess they went very carefully," she giggled.

Cra-tack!

Something sailed past Samantha's head, hit the closest display case, and bounced away. Startled, she looked around quickly and spotted a shiny object on the floor. She bent and picked it up. It was a metal half circle with numbers along each side.

"A protractor?" asked Samantha, holding it out for Nipper to see.

She and her brother had had a lot of things thrown

at them over the past few months. And it never meant anything good. She looked around the hallway, trying to spot where the protractor could have come from.

Cra-tack!

Something else bounced off the glass display case and dropped to the floor. More quickly than before, Samantha picked it up, too. The V-shaped object had a pencil on one end and a sharp metal needle on the other.

"A compass," said Samantha.

Cra-tack!

"A ruler," said Samantha, glancing at the floor again.

"Somebody really hates these knights in shining armor," said Nipper.

"Very funny," said Samantha, looking around. "But who's throwing these things at us?" Visitors had begun filtering into the museum. Men, women, and kids milled about the hall.

One couple in particular caught her eye. A man and a woman stood out from the rest of the crowd. They wore long white coats and bright white sneakers.

They looked exactly like the people Nipper had told her about—the ones who'd taken away Uncle Paul!

"Look," she said to Nipper, pointing at the couple.

"It's the math police!" her brother shouted.

Samantha watched them carefully. They stood facing her across the hall. She could *just* make out that the man had numbers on the front of his coat:

$$1+1=2$$

And on the woman's coat, she could see, there was an equation:

$$2+2=4$$

"I've already told you," she reminded her brother as she stared at the couple. "There's no such thing as the math police. They're the SNOW."

Abruptly the man and woman turned and began to run away.

"Don't let them get away," Samantha told Nipper, pointing her closed umbrella at them. "We need to ask them about—"

Thunk!

Another geometry compass flew past Samantha. The deadly sharp needle missed her face by inches and drove deep into the wooden handle of her umbrella.

She didn't care. This was her chance to find Uncle Paul. She took off toward the two figures in lab coats, chasing them down the grand hall.

"I'm right behind you, Sam," Nipper called.

Samantha was closing the distance between her and the SNOW when a line of people crossed in front of her, stopping her in her tracks. A dozen teenagers wearing matching yellow T-shirts meandered among the galleries. Their shirts said Tours du Jour on the front.

Samantha pushed her way through the line, trying to keep an eye on the man and woman.

"Excusez-moi," a teenage girl said to Samantha as she passed.

Samantha glanced at the girl. She looked familiar, but there wasn't time to stop and talk.

Samantha sprinted after the SNOW agents, but the hall had become crowded. Now that the guard had agreed to let visitors into the museum, hundreds of people moved in every direction.

Samantha hopped up and down to peek over the crowd and get a better view. She spotted the two white coats flashing through the crowd.

And then they were gone.

She searched the hall, but it was as if they'd disappeared.

"Don't stop, Sam," Nipper said. "I saw them go in

there!" He was pointing straight ahead, toward the two-story marble entrance they'd glimpsed earlier.

"Are you sure?" she asked.

He nodded.

She was going to have to trust that Nipper was actually paying attention to things this time. She nodded back, and together they sped toward the entrance.

CHAPTER TEN

TAKE ME TO THE RIVERA

Samantha and Nipper charged through the entrance-way, and they both stopped at the same time.

"Whoa, Nelly," said Nipper.

A vast indoor courtyard stretched out before them.

"The *Detroit Industry Murals*," Samantha said. "Uncle Paul told us about this last year."

"He did?" asked Nipper.

Samantha sighed.

"You were right there with me," she replied. "Uncle Paul told us all about this place . . . and *The Thinker* by Rodin . . . and . . ."

Her brother wasn't listening. He was staring at the walls of the courtyard.

Samantha guessed that the room was one hundred

feet long and at least forty feet high. And almost every inch of the four huge walls was covered with paintings, dozens of them. Most of the scenes showed men at work, building and operating machines, but others featured women and babies, fish and birds. Some paintings featured giant hands, rising from the ground, holding crystals. There were paintings of airplanes, doctors, and nurses, and a huge panel with a baby in a womb.

Two murals were bigger than the others. They presented scenes from a factory. Workers pushed and pulled machinery as they assembled cars. The paintings were fascinating and mysterious . . . and kind of gloomy, too. The people in these murals looked a little like machines, and several machines looked like people. One big machine looked like a giant human ear. Another looked like a human-shaped robot.

This was clearly one of the museum's main attractions. Dozens of men, women, and kids stood about, gazing in all directions. Like many of them, Samantha marveled at the colossal works of art.

Nipper tapped her on the shoulder.

"Uh-oh," he whispered, pointing to the center of the room. "Over there."

Two visitors weren't looking up at the paintings. They were staring at a cement planter along the wall that was holding a cluster of green plants a few feet beneath the bottom of one of the large murals.

"Math police," said Nipper.

Samantha didn't bother to correct him. She watched the woman in the lab coat reach into the planter.

Suddenly the man and the woman turned and pointed to the entrance of the room.

"Wow! Look over there!" they both yelled at the same time. "It's a famous billionaire internet movie star supermodel sports celebrity!"

All the visitors in the room turned to see who the famous celebrity might be.

Samantha turned to see, too.

She felt silly the moment she did. She knew there wasn't a famous billionaire internet movie star supermodel sports celebrity wandering through the crowd. It was a trick, and she'd fallen for it.

When she turned back, the SNOW people were gone.

The SNOW people were gone!

Samantha sighed as everyone went back to staring at the courtyard walls.

"You know, Sam," said Nipper, "I think the math police—I mean the SNOW—made that up about the movie star supermodel."

"Of course they did," she replied. "That was a distraction. Now help me figure out where they went."

Samantha looked back to where she'd last seen the SNOW—the planter. When she looked more closely, she saw something red poking out between green leaves.

"Come on," she said, and led her brother to the wall just beneath a section of the mural that showed a big machine.

She pushed away a plant leaf and realized immediately that it was a fake plastic plant.

"Just what I thought," she said. "There's no need for water."

In the planter, tucked between the plastic leaves, she had revealed a small faucet with a bright red knob poking out of the dirt.

"Go ahead," she told Nipper.

"I'm not really thirsty, Sam," he answered.

"You've got to be kidding me," said Samantha. "I show you a secret knob, on a mysterious faucet, probably hidden there by the SNOW, and you're not going to . . ."

Nipper had turned and was pointing at the entrance to the courtyard.

"Look!" he shouted. "It's the New York Yankees!"

Everyone in the room turned to see a Major League Baseball team.

Nipper looked at Samantha and winked. Then he pointed to the faucet.

Quickly she grabbed the red handle and gave it a twist.

Chunka-chunka-chunka!

Samantha looked up at the mural. One of the huge

machines that towered over the factory workers had begun to move.

A real machine had been hidden against the mural's painted machine scenery.

Clamp!

Clamp!

Two mighty robot arms reached out and grabbed Samantha and her brother.

Chunka!

A panel swung open, and the machine arms yanked both of them through the wall.

CHAPTER ELEVEN

WONDER AT THE WALL

Held fast in the mechanical arm's grasp, Samantha rocketed up, down, and around in darkness. She heard machinery clanking and grinding. It reminded her of the pneumatic tube ride under Paris—without the tube!

"Holy cow-a-bunga!" Nipper shouted somewhere next to her in the darkness.

Before she could call out to him, the ride was over.

Chunka!

Chunka!

The arms let go, dropping Samantha beside her brother onto the cement floor of a dimly lit chamber.

"Horrible!" shouted Nipper.

"Why do you say that?" asked Samantha. "I thought you liked roller coasters."

Nipper just grunted and pointed over her shoulder at the wall. Samantha turned around to see numbers set into the blocks of a grid that was seventeen squares long by nine squares wide.

1	1	2	3	4	5	6	7	8	9	10	11	12	13	14	15	16
17	18	19	20	21	22	23	24	25	26	27	28	29	30	31	32	33
34	35	36	37	38	39	40	41	42	43	44	45	46	47	48	49	50
51	52	53	54	55	56	57	58	59	60	61	62	63	64	65	66	67
68	69	70	71	72	73	74	75	76	77	78	79	80	81	82	83	84
85	86	87	88	89	90	91	92	93	94	95	96	97	98	99	100	101
102	103	104	105	106	107	108	109	110	111	112	113	114	115	116	117	118
119	120	121	122	123	124	125	126	127	128	129	130	131	132	133	134	135
136	137	138	139	140	141	142	143	144	145	146	147	148	149	150	151	152

On the floor, she spotted some faint, dusty footprints again. They led up to the wall and stopped.

"Salt prints again," she told her brother. "This must be a door of some kind."

"I told you," Nipper said, pulling himself to his feet and walking over to the grid. "Math is a big, fat barrier that blocks you from going where you want to, almost all the time."

"When did you say that?" she asked.

He didn't answer. Instead he reached out and pressed one of the squares, the number one hundred forty-four. It lit up.

But nothing else happened.

1	1	2	3	4	5	6	7	8	9	10	11	12	13	14	15	16
17	18	19	20	21	22	23	24	25	26	27	28	29	30	31	32	33
34	35	36	37	38	39	40	41	42	43	44	45	46	47	48	49	50
51	52	53	54	55	56	57	58	59	60	61	62	63	64	65	66	67
68	69	70	71	72	73	74	75	76	77	78	79	80	81	82	83	84
85	86	87	88	89	90	91	92	93	94	95	96	97	98	99	100	101
102	103	104	105	106	107	108	109	110	111	112	113	114	115	116	117	118
119	120	121	122	123	124	125	126	127	128	129	130	131	132	133	134	135
136	137	138	139	140	141	142	143	**144**	145	146	147	148	149	150	151	152

Samantha stared at the wall of numbers. Then she walked up to it and tapped a few of them. Each time she touched a square, its light turned on or off.

Still nothing happened.

"I'm not happy about this," she told her brother.

Nipper looked at her. Then began pressing button after button after button.

"What are you doing?" asked Samantha.

"There," said Nipper. "How about that? Are you happy?"

1	1	2	3	4	5	6	7	8	9	10	11	12	13	14	15	16
17	18	19	20	21	22	23	24	25	26	27	28	29	30	31	32	33
34	35	36	37	38	39	**40**	41	42	43	**44**	45	46	47	48	49	50
51	52	53	54	55	56	57	58	59	60	61	62	63	64	65	66	67
68	69	70	71	72	73	74	75	76	77	78	79	80	81	82	83	84
85	86	87	88	**89**	90	91	92	93	94	95	96	**97**	98	99	100	101
102	103	104	105	106	**107**	108	109	110	111	112	**113**	114	115	116	117	118
119	120	121	122	123	124	**125**	**126**	**127**	**128**	**129**	130	131	132	133	134	135
136	137	138	139	140	141	142	143	144	145	146	147	148	149	150	151	152

Nipper had pressed a combination of buttons to light up as a smiley face.

"Well . . . ," said Samantha, "it was a nice try."

It *was* a little funny, but not very helpful. Somehow, the SNOW—and Uncle Paul—had gone beyond this wall. She and her brother were at a dead end. She needed to go back to Seattle and think.

Samantha adjusted her umbrella on her shoulder. Then she glanced around and spotted a red faucet handle along the wall at knee height.

"Ready to go home?" she asked her brother.

"And save my Yankees," he answered.

Samantha sighed. Her brother had a one-track mind. She twisted the handle.

Chunk-a! Chunk-a!

Soon they were on their way, zipping, and looping, up to the museum . . . and back to the one-track mine.

CHAPTER TWELVE

LORE OF THE RING

As soon as the robot roller coaster dropped Samantha and Nipper back into the museum courtyard, they retraced their path through the museum. Then they headed down under *The Thinker,* through the salt mine, and onward to the *kogelbaan* station. Soon they were speeding back to Seattle inside a giant rolling marble.

Samantha felt disappointed . . . and salty. The first thing she'd do when she got home was wash her hands and face. She looked at her salty arms and legs. Then again, maybe she would take a shower.

She looked at her umbrella. The SNOW's compass stuck out of the handle. She yanked the sharp object free and put it into her purse. The second thing she'd do when she got home was research math weapons in her uncle's *Encyclopedia Missilium.*

She took out her journal and made a grid. Then she started filling in numbers.

1, 2, 3, 4, 5, 6, 7, 8, 9, 10, 11, 12, 13 . . .

There were so many numbers. The SNOW had some secret code or pattern to activate that light-up wall. She didn't know where to begin, and her uncle hadn't left her any clues.

Or had he?

"The pattern is in the plaid," she repeated softly.

Nipper tapped her on the shoulder.

"Hey, Sam," he said. "Did you figure out where the math police went?"

"They're not the math police," she said impatiently. "And, no. Not yet . . . so let me think."

Nipper leaned forward on the yellow leather bench of the giant marble.

"Maybe you need to sit like *this*," he suggested, propping his chin on his fist. He pretended to be *The Thinker.*

"Can't you even be serious for two minutes?" asked Samantha.

Nipper looked at her. A thoughtful expression swept across his face, and he dropped his hands to his sides. He took a deep breath.

"Okay," he told her. "I do have something to show you . . . and it's important."

She wasn't sure what was coming next, but her brother really *did* look serious.

Nipper reached into his pocket and pulled out a ring. It had a shiny green scorpion on the top. It blinked.

"Is that the bug ring you took from the Temple of Horus?" she asked. "Didn't you give it away to Missy Snoddgrass?"

"No, Sam," he said. "I got this ring from the CLOUD. I have to switch it with the one on Missy's finger, so my Yankees can—"

"Stop," said Samantha. "Are you still thinking about baseball?"

Nipper nodded slowly.

"We were just attacked by the math police . . . I mean the SNOW," she said. "We were hot on the trail of Uncle Paul when they got away and we got stuck. The pattern is in the plaid. And besides, you have far exceeded your time to rattle on and on about the Yankees."

Nipper sat next to her fidgeting with the ring. It looked like he started to slip it onto his finger, then stopped himself.

"We need to rescue Uncle Paul," said Samantha. "Forget about that bug ring."

"It's not a bug. It's an arachnid," said Nipper.

The ring blinked in Nipper's hands.

"It's a *fake* plastic arachnid," Samantha corrected him.

"I know this one's a fake," said her brother. "But there's a *real* one on Missy's finger. And now the Yankees are losing every game they play because of a terrible ancient curse."

"That curse is all in your mind," said Samantha. "The Yankees are just having a bad season."

"Time is running out," said Nipper, his voice rising. He started waving his hands dramatically. "My Yankees are in grave danger!"

"I get it," said Samantha. "I know you're really upset, but—"

"You don't get it at all, Sam," he replied.

Nipper stared at her, looking serious, for a long time. Then he turned and stared into the ball tunnel ahead of them.

"It hurts when the Yankees lose," he said. "But it *really* hurts . . . when you lose the Yankees."

CHAPTER THIRTEEN

VALUES

Absolute Value stood in the center of the dome and studied the big whiteboard. With a marker, he added up the SNOW's sales for the year.

Fake paintings:	$500,000
Fake sculptures:	$1,500,000
Fake jewels:	$1,000,000
Total income:	**$3,000,000**

He nodded to himself. The SNOW's crimes had brought in three million dollars. He smiled and looked off into the distance.

Blue sparks flew from tables where the jewelry team worked away. Sizzling and popping, the plasma carvers in their hands blazed and chopped at salt and quartz, as a fresh batch of fake diamonds and rubies took shape. A dozen of the best mathematical criminals in the world were hard at work, applying geometry to forgery.

He looked in another direction. Twenty agents hammered and chipped, making quality imitations of famous sculptures. The team calculated, measured, and carved. A fresh new copy of Michelangelo's *David* was almost complete.

Absolute smiled again. Then he peered around at the edges of the dome. Far away, a team of agents packed up fake treasures and loaded them onto mine carts.

Another team polished sculptures, getting them ready for shipment.

He looked over to the booth containing the man in the green plaid pajamas. Another SNOW team was busy interrogating the mysterious man inside the big, glass box.

Another team stitched and repaired torn lab coats.

Another team popped popcorn.

Another team sharpened pencils.

He wrinkled his brow. That was a lot of teams. There were a whole lot of Super-Numerical Overachievers Worldwide.

He looked up at the big whiteboard and started writing again.

Uniforms:	$100,000
Markers, pens, and pencils:	$100,000
Rulers and compasses:	$50,000
Electricity:	$750,000
Trucks:	$900,000
Gas and highway tolls:	$100,000
Dome building and upkeep:	$500,000
Mine cart operations:	$490,000
Snacks:	$9,995
Total expenses:	**$2,999,995**
Total profits for the year:	**$5**

"Five dollars?" grumbled Absolute. "That's all?"

He heard footsteps approaching from the entrance tunnel and looked up to see two agents running in.

"Hey, boss!" someone called. "We just ran away from two kids!"

Absolute turned around. It was Agents 1+1=2 and 2+2=4.

"You're interrupting my math time to tell me you're scared of children?" he barked at them.

"No, boss," panted 1+1=2. "We ran here to tell you about them."

"Can't you see I'm busy?" growled Absolute.

He looked down at the two agents. At six and a half feet tall, he towered over them. They looked up at him nervously.

"We were up in the Detroit Institute of Arts," said 2+2=4. "We saw a girl with a red—"

"I don't care what kind of things you saw in the museum!" snapped Absolute. "I'm busy trying to solve our money problems!"

He turned back to face the whiteboard.

"But, boss," one of them pleaded. "The girl was carrying a—"

"Go away!" he shouted without turning around.

He stared at the board while he listened to the sound of the SNOW agents walking away. Then he turned and looked over at the prisoner in the glass booth.

The interrogation team had better get some answers out of the man in the green pajamas soon.

According to the clowns, ninjas, and others, Pajama Paul Spinner knew all kinds of ways to travel secretly around the world. He even had a super-super-secret map somewhere, with super-secret plans printed on the inside of a red umbrella.

If he could get his hands on that map, they could ditch the salt trucks and the fake weather alerts. They could sneak around the world, cheaply, quickly . . . and finally start making a profit!

Absolute glanced at the interrogation team again. They were walking around the booth. None of them looked happy. Some of the agents had their heads down. They all seemed frustrated.

The man in the both stood there, smiling peacefully.

The big SNOW boss sighed.

If only the man in the green plaid pajamas would stop being so mysterious and give them some straightforward answers!

CHAPTER FOURTEEN

WATCH OUT FOR THE SNOW

After a quick shower and a change of clothes, Samantha felt much better.

Salt-free, she sat down at her desk and opened the large, hardcover book with the words *Encyclopedia Missilium* engraved on the cover.

Her uncle kept a whole range of odd and often-confusing books on the shelves in his apartment, and this encyclopedia was the oddest and most confusing of them all.

In the past, it had been helpful . . . but not always super-helpful.

Samantha had borrowed it a month ago to research the terrible clowns known as the SUN, and last week to research metal boomerangs and the daredevils known as the CLOUD. The book still sat on her desk.

She flipped forward and backward through the pages until she spotted a drawing of a compass. Then she turned back one page to the start of the chapter.

"Chapter nineteen," she read. "Weapons of math destruction."

KILLER COMPASSES, RUTHLESS RULERS, AND PROTRACTOR PROJECTILES

Razor-sharp math tools are deadly weapons in the hands of the Super-Numerical Over-achievers Worldwide, aka the SNOW.

This team of ninety-nine mathematicians has mastered addition, subtraction, multiplication . . . and imitation. They use their skills to forge famous artwork, including paintings, sculptures, and jewelry. Then they swap them with real treasures—and almost no one notices.

The SNOW creates fake weather alerts to cover their movement around the country and allow for their thievery to go unnoticed. They broadcast news of bogus blizzards, fictional frosts, and invented ice storms to distract, and they use salt trucks as transportation, relying on the assumption that the trucks are there to salt the roads. The SNOW then steals treasures and leaves forgeries in their place, and no one realizes that a crime has been committed.

To date, the SNOW has used their fake alerts and forgeries to rob museums and galleries only in the United States. However, if they could find a secret way to travel around the world, then no museum, gallery, or private collection would be safe from their tricks, or their razor-sharp blades.

The SNOW's headquarters is located underneath an art museum somewhere in the United States. Even if you can find it, you won't be able to get in unless you know their *secret sequence.*

See also CALCU-LASERS, PLASMA CARVERS

"Secret sequence," said Samantha out loud.

Slam!

She closed the book a little harder than she'd intended.

She had traced the SNOW to their headquarters, *almost.* She had gotten all the way to their secret number wall. But she definitely didn't know the secret sequence that would get her inside.

"The pattern is in the plaid," she said once again.

Clearly Uncle Paul knew all about the SNOW and their secret headquarters. He'd left the worn mitten and the salt as clues so she would follow him. But how was she supposed to find the pattern when he was *wearing* the plaid?

She was stuck in a brand-new mystery from Uncle Paul! What did he think she was . . . a master detective?

Samantha put her face in her hands for a moment. Then it hit her.

"Master detective," she said thoughtfully.

She grabbed her journal, got up from her desk, opened the door to her room, and headed downstairs. In the kitchen, she picked up the phone and called the only master detective she knew.

"Hi, Fiona," she said. "It's Samantha."

CHAPTER FIFTEEN

FROM PLAID TO WORSE

Almost everyone in Seattle—between the ages five and fourteen—knew Fiona Hill. She was brilliant, and she was a master detective. She helped people find lost pets, remember passwords, and solve puzzles of every type. She was a scavenger hunt champ, and an escape room superstar.

The last time Samantha had seen her, Fiona had helped track down Nipper in the *kogelbaan*. Samantha couldn't have found her brother without Fiona's help. It was also fun to be with someone her age who was interested in a lot of the same things, for once.

Fiona was one of the few people Samantha's age who knew several languages, and had experience solving mysteries around the world. She even went to *detective train camp,* where private eye campers rolled around Europe solving mysteries. Today was a good excuse for Samantha to call her. And she really needed her help, too.

"Hello, Samantha Spinner," said Fiona when she answered the phone.

It was hard to tell if Fiona was being formal or just organized.

"Hi," Samantha answered. "I need a secret sequence, and I'm stuck."

"Okay," said "Fiona. "Can you share any more details?"

"That's the problem," said Samantha. "All I have are the numbers from one to one hundred fifty-three. They're on a wall."

"Wall?" asked Fiona.

"I'm pretty sure that wall is some kind of giant keypad-doorway for people to open," said Samantha.

"People?" asked Fiona. "Anyone I know?"

"I doubt it," said Samantha. "They call themselves the SNOW."

"Interesting," said Fiona. "*Snow* keeps coming up a lot lately, even though it's the middle of summer."

Samantha wasn't sure just how many details she wanted to share with Fiona. She planned to tell Fiona all about the umbrella and her secret travels around the world, someday. But she wasn't ready to do that quite yet. Uncle Paul was pretty careful about protecting super secrets. She got the sense that he wanted her to be careful, too.

"It's amazing how many people will believe things without checking the facts," said Fiona. "Like these fake storm alerts we've been getting. They're ridiculous."

"I agree completely," said Samantha.

Maybe she should tell Fiona about the security guard outside the museum in Detroit.

"Do you want to come over and help me figure out the pattern?" Samantha asked.

"Oh," said Fiona. "I'd really like to, but I'm heading out of town tonight. Some kids in Botswana are building the world's trickiest escape room. They're flying me there to try to break it. I have to pack this afternoon while I practice my Tswana."

"Tswana?" asked Samantha.

"That's the most common language in Botswana, spoken by five million people," said Fiona.

"Oh," said Samantha, disappointed.

"I'll give you a call and tell you all about it when I get back," said Fiona.

This made Samantha feel a little bit better.

"Maybe you could spend time exploring your brother's brain on this subject," said Fiona. "From what you've told me, he might be able to come up with a plan of some kind."

"Thanks. . . . I will," said Samantha.

"*Tsamaya sentle,*" said Fiona. "That's 'goodbye' in Tswana."

Samantha said goodbye in English and hung up.

She picked up the mitten. Salt sprinkled out onto the table again.

She had ridden through a dusty salt mine. She'd explored a sewage-flooded tomb. She'd been chased though crowded noisy markets, dropped onto water slides, and squeezed through pneumatic tubes.

None of that would be as awful as exploring Nipper's New York Yankees–filled brain.

CHAPTER SIXTEEN

DISMISSY

Samantha sat at the kitchen table, studying the number grid in her journal. She heard footsteps and a scraping noise. Nipper marched past her, stopped at the side door, and called back.

"Let's go," he said.

Samantha stared at him. Her brother was wearing a strange helmet. It looked like an upside-down flowerpot made of leather, and he was dragging a baseball bat along the kitchen floor.

"What's on your head?" she asked.

"I got an old football helmet from Uncle Paul," he answered. "It's for extra protection."

"And what's that you're holding?" asked Samantha.

"I told you," said Nipper. "We need extra protection where we're going."

"Going?" she asked. "Where do you think we're going?"

"Next door," he answered. "This is a mission to get my Yankees back."

"Oh, come on," she replied. "Haven't you learned anything?"

"No, I haven't," said Nipper. "And time's running out."

He walked back and forth, dragging the bat on the kitchen floor.

"I only have three games left to break the curse," he said.

"And how exactly are you planning to break a curse with a baseball bat and a football helmet?" Samantha asked.

"I already told you," said Nipper. "I'm going to break the curse by getting the ring back."

He pointed out the kitchen window with the bat.

"Do you see that green light blinking on the Snodd-grasses' back porch?" he asked. "I think that's the scorpion ring. Missy must take it off her finger at night."

Samantha turned and looked out the window, squinting at their neighbors' backyard. Something sparkled through the porch screen . . . *maybe*. She couldn't be sure.

She looked at her brother again. He had raised the bat behind his head as if waiting to swing at a baseball.

"That's why I've got this extra protection, see?" Nipper added. "I don't want to get caught in another ball of yarn or anything like that."

Samantha just stared at him. She didn't say anything. She was confident this was going to end badly. There was no point in dragging out the conversation.

"So?" asked Nipper.

"So, what?" she replied.

"So are you coming with me?" he said.

"No, Nipper," said Samantha. "I'm not going with you."

"Why not?" Nipper asked.

"For a dozen reasons," she answered.

"Name one," said Nipper.

"I'm busy," said Samantha.

"Oh, come on, Sam," he pleaded. "Tell me one thing that is more important than saving my Yankees."

"I just did," she replied. "I can't go with you right now, because I'm *busy* trying to figure out this math puzzle."

"Arrrrgh," Nipper growled. "Math keeps destroying my life. . . . It never ends."

"I also don't want to be seen anywhere near you right now," she said. "You look ridiculous."

Nipper pulled off his football helmet and scowled.

"Fine. Why else not?" he asked.

"I'm not going with you because it will be a big waste of time," said Samantha. "We both know that you're going to hop over the bushes between our houses. Then you're not going to get what you want from Missy Snoddgrass. You're going to make that face like your head is about to explode. *Then* you won't feel like hopping over the bushes, so you'll trudge all the way down the driveway and around to our front door . . . and I don't have time to join you through all of that right now."

Nipper waited.

"Why else?" he asked.

"Because this is completely foolish!" Samantha shouted. "I've already told you: There's no such thing as a magic evil curse. It's just an ugly bug ring. Don't try to drag me into your silly *mission*."

"Fine," said Nipper, lowering his bat so that it clunked on the floor. "My Yankees need me, and I'm the only person in the world who cares."

He opened the kitchen door and started to leave. Then he turned back.

"And I told you before," he added. "It's not a bug. It's an arachnid. Scorpions and spiders are arachnids."

CHAPTER SEVENTEEN

MISSION: UNCROSSABLE

Nipper hopped over the bushes that ran between his house and the Snoddgrass lair. He glanced left and right. The driveway was clear.

Clunk! Clunk! Clun—

He adjusted his grip on the baseball bat to keep it from knocking against the pavement.

He stepped lightly, trying to make as little noise as possible.

All the windows on both floors of the house were dark. The only light Nipper could see was a faint green flicker on the back porch.

The mission was going exactly as planned.

He glanced to his left as he walked past the Snodd-grass garage.

He stopped.

The setting summer sun bathed the sky in orange and purple light. The shifting colors . . . made the garage look strange.

In the light of day, the building at the end of Missy's driveway didn't look remarkable in any way. He had never even noticed it.

Now, with the orange-and-purple tint of the sunset, patches of shadows and colors stood out and Nipper could see things more clearly. He looked more closely at the garage and realized it was actually a huge knitted curtain.

"Camouflage?" Nipper said curiously.

He stared. With the sun low on the horizon, he could *just* see the outline of something big sitting behind the garage curtain.

"A ship?" said Nipper, squinting at the shape. Could Missy be hiding a giant boat in her fake garage?

"I better remember this for later," said Nipper. "I'm sure Sam would really want to know there's a . . ."

Nipper was distracted by a flash of red and blue.

". . . a parrot," he finished.

It was Sammy. Nipper's feathered foe. His avian enemy. His *nemesis*.

The bird perched on the handle of a shovel stuck into the ground, blocking the path to Missy's back porch. It didn't move. Its eyes were closed. Was it asleep?

Nipper watched Sammy carefully as he began to tip-toe toward it.

He got closer to the bird. . . . He was right beside it. . . . He was starting to pass it. . . .

Suddenly the parrot's eyelids opened. Nipper froze.

"Annoying boy! Annoying boy!" it squawked loudly.

"Hush," said Nipper, waggling a finger at the bird.

Snap!

The parrot pinched Nipper's finger with the tip of its beak and, "Yow!" he shouted. The bite wasn't hard enough to break the skin, but it sure hurt!

Nipper pulled his hand back as lights turned on in all the windows of the house.

The mission was not going as planned.

Nipper started to raise the baseball bat, and *bonk!* The parrot sailed forward and crashed into his shoulder. Nipper lost his grip on the baseball bat and he dropped it to the ground.

"Strike one!" Sammy squawked.

Nipper bent and reached to pick up the bat.

Bonk! Sammy flew into Nipper's chest, bumping him backward and sending him to the ground.

"Strike two!" the parrot shouted.

Nipper stood up and glared at the bird.

Suddenly it began to flap its wings furiously. It shot straight into the air.

The bird was very high . . . and now it was diving straight down at him!

"Strike three!" Sammy called.

Nipper faced straight ahead, gritted his teeth, and prepared for impact. He was glad he'd worn the old football helmet from Uncle Paul.

Thump!

The bird slammed into the heavily padded center of the top of the leather helmet, and . . . it didn't hurt at all.

Nipper smiled.

"Extra protection," he said.

Ba-da-ba-da-ba-da!

The parrot began hammering away at the not-so-padded side of Nipper's head like a mad woodpecker.

Ba-da-ba-da-ba-da!

And *that* hurt a lot!

Ba-da-ba-da-ba-da!

Ba-da-ba-da-ba-da!

Ba-da-ba-da-ba-da!

Nipper tried to swat the bird, but it fluttered around his head, hammering and pecking at the helmet.

"Yahhhhhh!" Nipper wailed. He flailed his free arm to try to stop the bird, but the parrot hammered away.

Nipper thought of the llama he'd met near Machu Picchu. The one that had bashed him on the shoulder, then knocked him down and dragged him across the ground and kicked rocks and pebbles at him.

This hurt two point four billion times worse than that had!

Ba-da-ba-da-ba-da!

"Yaaaaaah!" Nipper wailed.

He dropped the baseball bat and began waving both of his arms wildly around his head until the bird hopped off.

Samantha had been wrong about one thing: Nipper wasn't going to trudge down the Snoddgrass driveway. . . . He was going to run!

Nipper tossed the useless old helmet at the bird and began sprinting down the driveway. He raced around to the front of the Spinner residence, opened the door, and slammed it behind him before the bird could hammer him again.

"Yankees lose!" Sammy the parrot cackled. *"Yankees are the worst! The worst! The worst!"*

CHAPTER EIGHTEEN

CALL IN THE FAMILY

The next day Dr. Suzette Spinner spent all morning supervising deliveries. When Buffy had gone to California, she left thousands of things behind in her New York apartment. Now, box after box of accessories, artwork, and decorations streamed in from trucks. By the early afternoon, everything was stacked neatly in the Spinner garage.

Dr. Spinner headed into the kitchen and leaned against the counter. She fanned herself with a clipboard. She was exhausted.

Samantha was *still* at the kitchen table, staring at her journal. Had she even gone to bed last night? She seemed to be staring at a grid of numbers.

"It's a beautiful day, dear," said Dr. Spinner. "You should go outside and enjoy it."

Samantha kept staring at her journal.

Clack!

Mrs. Spinner dropped the clipboard onto the counter, and Samantha looked up.

"I'm sorry," said Samantha. "Did you say something to me, Mom?"

"Why don't you take a little break?" asked Dr. Spinner. "It's not raining—or snowing, for that matter—and . . . and . . ."

Samantha had gone back to staring at her journal again.

Dr. Spinner sighed and picked up a pen. She straightened the clipboard and began to review Buffy's cargo checklist.

"Pool table . . . ten pinball machines . . . robot massage chair . . . ," she read down the list. "Motorized spin art wheel . . . exercise equipment . . ."

Nipper stomped into the kitchen from the living room. His hair was a mess, and he looked very angry.

"Is everything all right with you?" Dr. Spinner asked him.

Nipper crossed his arms and didn't say a word. Then he slowly turned to face Samantha, and scowled.

"Sometimes I wish I had capybaras instead of kids," said Dr. Spinner.

She waited for Samantha and Nipper to react. Neither of them did. She went back to the checklist.

"Top hat . . . old-fashioned movie theater popcorn popper . . ."

The phone rang. Nipper grabbed it.

"Spinner house," he announced. "Home of the unhelpful sister."

"Cease your baby talk!" Buffy's voice barked from the phone. *"I need help! Let me speak to Mother!"*

Nipper flinched and held out the phone.

"It's Buffy. I think she's screaming for you, Mom," he said.

Dr. Spinner looked over at the kitchen table.

"Samantha," she said. "Be a dear and help your sister for me."

"Does she need help traveling to Antarctica and not coming back?" Samantha replied. "Otherwise, I'd really prefer not to. And I mean really, really, really, really, really, really—"

Dr. Spinner pointed two fingers at Samantha and made eye contact. It was her professional-strength veterinarian gaze. She used it when she needed to make rodents and lizards calm down and do what she wanted them to do.

Nipper handed the phone to Samantha.

Samantha took it from Nipper.

"Hi, Buffy," she said into the phone. "How are things in California?"

CHAPTER NINETEEN

HOLLYWOOD BAWL

"Sammy?" Buffy's voice screeched from the phone. "Is that you?"

Samantha didn't reply. She really hated it when anyone called her *Sammy*.

She needed to find Uncle Paul.

She *didn't* need to find out about her older sister's latest ridiculousness.

She didn't need to hear about her big-budget movie . . . which had gotten turned into a Broadway play . . . which had gotten turned into a musical nature documentary.

Samantha looked back at her mother, who was still pointing at her with two fingers, veterinarian-style.

Samantha sighed.

"Okay," she said into the phone. "How's the nature documentary coming?"

"*Scarlett Hydrangea's Wild, Wild Secret of the Nile* is far from fabulous," said her sister. "The makeup crew is on strike. No one wants to put foundation on the porcupines. Every time I yell *Action,* all the pangolins roll into balls. And when the spotlights come on, the nocturnal animals go to sleep."

"I understand," said Samantha.

"Of course you do," said Buffy. "Everyone here is a complete fashion disaster like you. And my stars can't learn their lines."

"Stars?" asked Samantha. "When you say *stars,* you mean animals, right?"

She didn't really care about her sister's animals *or* stars, but she was going to have to listen, or she was never going to get off the phone and get back to finding Uncle Paul.

"They *could* be stars," said Buffy. "If they'd only stop scratching themselves and start practicing my choreography."

"Choreography," said Samantha, trying to sound interested. "You're trying to teach animals how to dance?"

"That's only one of my problems," Buffy answered. "We put the chameleons in front of a green screen, and now we can't find them. And don't even get me started on the Gila monster. I tried to put a cute little hat with a pink bow on its head . . . and it bit me! Fifteen times! I just sent the crew out shopping for Band-Aids. They have to find a lot of different colors to match all the outfits I'm going to wear to all the award ceremonies."

Samantha glanced at her mother. Dr. Spinner was still pointing two fingers at her.

"You really think your movie is going to win awards?" Samantha asked into the phone.

"It would . . . if it weren't so behind schedule," Buffy continued. "We lost a week of filming because of the blizzard."

"Blizzard?" asked Samantha. "In Southern California? In August?"

Samantha didn't believe it. It sounded like another fake weather alert from the SNOW.

"It's was horrible," her sister explained. "We all had to stock up on shovels and warm clothes. There were salt trucks everywhere."

"Sure," said Samantha. "But did you actually see any clouds or precipitation?"

"No," said Buffy. "But all of Hollywood stayed indoors because of the SCOW—the Southern California Outside Warning."

Samantha heard Buffy sniffle several times, then a half dozen times more. She thought it sounded like

Dennis, sniffing the floor in search of waffles, but she decided not to mention it. She wanted to hear if there were any clues about the SNOW.

"It doesn't matter anyway," Buffy continued. "*Scarlett Hydrangea's Wild, Wild Secret of the Nile* still doesn't have a real unicorn. The director rented a llama from Mali, but it's not fooling anyone."

"Mali?" asked Samantha. "Are you sure you don't mean Lima?"

Samantha thought of her recent trip to Lima, Peru. Her brother had gotten attacked by a very angry llama near there. She was pretty sure there weren't any llamas in Mali . . . in Africa—

"I don't care," said Buffy. "They glued a foam rubber horn onto the llama's head. It's really mad about it!"

Buffy was sniffling and breathing heavily, and Samantha hoped Buffy wasn't going to start full-blown crying. That would make this phone call even longer for sure.

"It's all so embarrassing!" Buffy wailed. "If I come back to dreary Seattle, I'm not even sure I'll include it in my *Unicorn-O-Pedia!*"

"*Unicorn-O-Pedia?*" asked Samantha. This was new.

"Yes," Buffy answered. "I've been working on it for a few years. I keep it by my bedside in my room, on my nightstand. When it's done, I'm going to get it published.

It will have a pink cover—no, a rainbow cover. And it will have sparkly gems and gold letters."

"What is it, exactly?" asked Samantha.

"It's my complete compendium of fabulousness," said Buffy. "I figured that's where you got the idea for that gloomy diary of yours. It's kind of sweet, actually, when your little sister tries to copy you. You must really look up to me."

"Copy you?" asked Samantha angrily. "I don't copy . . . and I certainly don't look up to you."

"Of course, *your* version is filled with drab buildings and notes about crowded, smelly transportation," said Buffy. "And all those dreary poems about Nelly McPepper. Dreary and pointless."

"It's not pointless," said Samantha. "It's a *journal*. I'm filling it with all the special things I've learned from Uncle Paul."

"Oh, he's helped me add some things, too," said Buffy. "He told me it was important to include some special entries. Flip-flops and flannel. Plaid, pajamas, patterns."

Samantha gasped. Had Uncle Paul left clues with Buffy about the pattern in the . . .

"Wait!" snapped Samantha, suddenly realizing what her sister had been doing. "You've been reading my journal?"

"You left it where anyone could read it," said Buffy.

"Under the shredded paper in the stable, inside your suitcase, wrapped in one of those hideous horizontal-striped shirts you always wear."

When Samantha and Nipper had stayed in New York, they'd been forced to stay in her sister's stables that were meant for unicorns.

"Buffy!" Samantha shouted into the phone.

"Black and white isn't a good look for you, you know," said Buffy. "Maybe you should order some custom fabric, like Uncle Paul."

"Custom fabric?" Samantha asked. This was the first time she'd heard anything about custom fabric.

"Weren't you listening?" asked Buffy. "Uncle Paul told me to write about plaid pajama patterns in my *Unicorn-O-Pedia*. Of course, he's a total fashion disaster. I wish there were some way I could convince you to—"

"Stop," said Samantha.

She turned to her mother. She had to get off this call and see what Uncle Paul had told Buffy to add to her silly unicorn journal.

"Mom!" she said. "Are Gila monsters poisonous?"

Dr. Spinner nodded.

"I'm handing you over to a real animal expert," Samantha told her sister, and she held out the phone to her mom. "I think you better talk to Buffy, Mom." she said. "Ask her about her lizard bites."

Dr. Spinner took the phone from her, noticeably alarmed.

Samantha left the kitchen and raced up the stairs to Buffy's room and checked her sister's nightstand for a *Unicorn-O-Pedia*.

CHAPTER TWENTY

SCARLET HYDRANGEA'S UNICORN-O-PEDIA

Samantha walked into Buffy's bedroom and went right to her sister's nightstand. She spotted a pink book that sparkled with gems and gold letters, just like Buffy had described.

"Volume two," she said, reading the cover. "Jewelry to Sapphire."

She sat down at the foot of her sister's bed and opened the book. She flipped ahead to the words beginning with the letter P:

Pair
A set of two: More than one and less than three. A pair of siblings (a sister and a little

baby brother, for example) can be very annoying. They tend to rattle on about their boring lives. A pair of rainbow unicorns, however, is the most beautiful thing in the world.

Pajamas
The clothes you wear at night when you go to bed. Or, if you are a fashion disaster, the clothes you wear outside during the day when you want to embarrass the other members of your family. Unicorns do not wear pajamas.

Pancakes
Round things that clowns throw when they are running around your theater and messing up your fabulous Broadway play. Unicorns prefer candy corn.

Pattern
An arrangement of shapes, such as squares or stripes. Some people order custom pattern material from local fabric stores. They might be hiding special information in the lines. Of course, that would just make the clothes look even more hideous. It would also take time away from shopping for unicorns.

Pegasus
A Pegasus is NOT a unicorn. A Pegasus is a smelly horse with wings. Remember that when you are out shopping for rainbow unicorns.

Peru
One of the places where llamas can be found. Some people might try to dress up a llama with a fake foam rubber horn and then try to convince you that it's a unicorn. Don't be fooled!

Pirate
A person who waves a sword around and says things like "Arrrrr," "Ahoy, Matey," or "No, Buffy. There be no unicorns here."

Pittsburgh
A city in Pennsylvania. They have a baseball team called *the Pirates*. Their mascot is not a unicorn.

Plaid
Squares and lines on cloth. Plaid clashes terribly with rainbow unicorns. See PATTERN. . . . Or a fashion advisor!

Platinum

Unicorn horns and pirate swords scratch gold ceilings too easily. Platinum is a metal that provides extra protection.

Procrastinate

To put off something that you need to do right away. If you procrastinate going to school, your mother might get angry, cancel your Broadway play, and refuse to help you shop for unicorns.

Procrasti-Nate

An unreliable assistant who promises to help shop for unicorns but fails miserably. If he starts talking like a pirate and attacks your family, you'll need a Komodo dragon to make him stop.

Pug

A little dog with a round, flat face. According to some people, pugs are heroes that always save the day when you really need help. Maybe they sense moments of greatness. Maybe they want to save their friends. Or maybe it's because they are always trying to get a waffle, or a granola bar, or even

some chocolate. Unicorns require less main-
tenance.

Purple
Purple is the worst possible color for a pair
of sunglasses. Fashion disaster! Never, under
any circumstances, put purple sunglasses on
your rainbow unicorn. If someone is wearing a pair of spectacles with that color, there
must be a reason. Maybe the hideous custom fabric patterns pre-ordered by "Flip-flop
P. Wafflemaker" at Seattle Fabric Center look
better viewed through purple lenses.

"The pattern is in the plaid," murmured Samantha.
She closed the book and set it down on Buffy's desk.
Her heart was racing. If she could see the custom pat-
tern in her uncle's pajamas, she'd have a clue!
Samantha stood up, hurried to her own bedroom,
and grabbed the purple sunglasses Uncle Paul had given
her a few weeks ago. Then she headed downstairs to
the kitchen.
She dialed the phone.
No one answered, so she left a message.
"Hi, Lainey. It's me, Samantha," she said. "I need
you to meet me first thing in the morning . . . at Seattle
Fabric Center. . . ."

CHAPTER TWENTY-ONE

FABRICATED

Lainey Jain was the other friend who had helped Samantha when Nipper had been lost in the *kogelbaan*. She was nearly as brilliant as Fiona Hill, but her expertise centered almost entirely on one topic: little brothers.

Lainey knew everything that kid brothers liked, said, ate, read, collected, broke, lost, interrupted, and did and didn't pick up.

But that wasn't why Samantha called Lainey this time. She just wanted a smart friend to help her figure out SNOW's math wall . . . so she could get past it and find Uncle Paul!

* * *

When Samantha reached the Seattle Fabric Center the next day, Lainey was there, waiting for her outside on the street.

"Look at you," said Lainey. "Still carrying that umbrella, even on a sunny day."

"I'm so glad you got my message," Samantha said, ignoring Lainey's umbrella comment.

"I was home," said Lainey. "I just couldn't answer the phone. I was busy giving my chinchillas a dust bath."

"Chinchillas?" asked Samantha. "Plural?"

Samantha had a ton of experience with more than one chinchilla. Nipper had ordered one gross of them a few weeks ago. It was super-annoying.

"Yes," said Lainey. "My parents ordered one for me as a pet. I think they did it because they thought it would make up for me not having a sibling."

Samantha nodded. She imagined Lainey pestered her parents with that fact all the time.

"But then a *dozen* chinchillas showed up at the house," Lainey continued. "It's fun, but it's a ton of work."

Samantha nodded sympathetically, then got down to business.

"I'm here because of something my sister, Buffy, told me about."

"Your sister?" asked Lainey. "Isn't she kind of your *frenemy*?"

Samantha thought about Buffy Spinner: Whiner. Whimperer. Former billionaire. Misguided moviemaker. Failed Broadway producer. Fashion critic. Younger-sister critic. Younger-sister tormenter. Shoe hoarder. Younger-sister insulter. Younger-sister—

"No," Samantha answered. "She's much more than a frenemy. I don't think anyone's invented the right word for it yet."

She looked at the front door of Seattle Fabric Center. Last time she'd entered this place, it had been to get away from the ninjas of the Royal Academy of International Ninjas. Now she was heading back inside to find the pattern in the plaid.

Samantha reached for the door, but stopped when she saw a sign taped to the glass:

KNITTING WORKSHOP
SOLD OUT!
GLOVE AND PARKA PATTERNS
OUT OF STOCK!
DOGGIE SWEATER DESIGNS
DON'T ASK!

"Can you believe it?" asked Lainey. "All it takes is a mysterious warning, and people start preparing for an emergency that doesn't make any sense."

Samantha nodded. She agreed completely, but she

wasn't ready to tell Lainey what she had learned about the SNOW. She knew the time would come soon to tell her new friend everything about her uncle . . . and her Super-Secret Plans. But this wasn't the time.

"Come on," said Samantha, pushing open the door.

They headed to the front counter, where a woman sat, knitting busily.

"Hello," said Samantha. "I'm here to pick up a custom order."

"Name, please," said the woman, without looking up.

"Flip-Flop P. Wafflemaker," said Samantha.

"Who?" whispered Lainey.

"It's a long story," Samantha whispered back. "Trust me."

"No problem," the woman answered, setting down her knitting.

She opened a cabinet underneath the counter and began to search through it.

"Ah," said the woman. "It's right—" She stopped.

The woman was no longer looking in the cabinet, though. She was staring at Samantha's umbrella.

"I'm sorry," said the woman slowly. "There's no order under that name."

"What?" asked Lainey. "You were just about to—"

The woman moved her arms under the counter.

Bzzzzzzzzzzeerrrrrnnnnnt!

"What was that?" asked Lainey.

"Oh, that?" replied the clerk. "I'm doing some document shredding. You can't be too careful with personal information these days."

"I know," said Lainey, getting distracted. "A lot of people have little brothers, and they love to snoop around in other people's—"

"Wait," Samantha said. "Are you sure there's no custom plaid here?"

"I'm positive," said the woman.

"Hold on!" Samantha interrupted. "Are you shredding the pattern I asked for?"

"Nope," said the woman. "It turns out I was mistaken. I couldn't find your pattern. This is just some old wrapping paper or a receipt or something that isn't your custom plaid pattern."

Samantha's heart was racing. Her plan was falling apart. She had been about to get an important clue . . . and then the woman had shredded it!

"Could you please double-check for us?" Lainey asked.

The woman stood up.

"I'd love to," she answered. "But we're closing. There's a big winter storm on the way."

Lainey looked like she was about to argue, but Samantha touched her shoulder.

"Forget it," she said. "I can tell this will go nowhere."

Samantha was tired. Her clue was shredded, and so

was her chance of finding Uncle Paul. She didn't want to spend another minute in the Seattle Fabric Center. She waved for Lainey to follow her and left the store.

"That was strange," said Lainey as they walked back down Broadway, toward Aloha Street. "Do you think that woman shredded that paper to stop you from discovering something?"

"I think so," said Samantha. "Or maybe not."

This was another dead end.

"Nobody's helping me these days," said Samantha.

She made eye contact with Lainey.

"Except for you, of course," she added.

They passed Coffee Mania. A sign in the window of the café said:

BLIZZARD SPECIAL:
DOUBLE YOUR FOAM—THEN RUN FOR HOME!

Samantha shook her head. Her hopes where shredded.

"I feel like Nelly McPepper," said Samantha.

"Who?" Lainey asked.

"She was the girl my sister didn't take to California," said Samantha. "Because she wore white after Labor Day."

"You're not supposed to do that?" asked Lainey.

Samantha thought about it. She had to admit it was a silly rule.

"Well, in my sister's world," said Samantha, "it's a major-league rule."

"So," said Lainey. "Is Nelly McPepper a friend of yours?"

Samantha shrugged. "Not really," she answered. "I've never actually met her."

"Does she live in Seattle?" asked Lainey.

"Maybe," said Samantha. "I'm not sure what happened to her. I've been pretty focused on trying to find my uncle these days. And if I can't figure out that plaid pattern, then I'm stuck."

Lainey looked at Samantha for a moment. She seemed to be thinking things over.

"Is your little brother home?" she asked.

"Probably," said Samantha. "He's got a big problem of his own he's working on."

"Have you considered helping him with his problem, so he can help you with yours?" Lainey asked.

"I *knew* you were going to say that!" Samantha snapped. "The answer is . . . no! He's completely ridiculous. And super-annoying."

"Okay, okay," said Lainey. "It was just a suggestion."

"And besides," Samantha continued, "he doesn't know any information that I don't already have!"

She realized she was shouting at her friend and stopped. She took a deep breath.

"I'm sorry, Lainey," said Samantha. "I'm just disappointed that my plans here got . . ."

"Shredded?" Lainey suggested.

"Yeah," said Samantha, smirking just a little.

They reached the corner where their paths split.

"Promise you won't forget about my party this Saturday," said Lainey.

"I won't," said Samantha.

She was glad Lainey had reminded her. She had been so focused on her plaid problem that she *had* almost forgotten about the party invitation. And it was good to hear that Lainey still wanted her to come, even though Samantha had just yelled at her.

"Hold on," said Lainey. "I've got it."

"What?" asked Samantha. "The plaid pattern?"

"No," Lainey replied. "I've invented a word to describe your sister."

Samantha waited.

"She's your *neme-sister*," said Lainey.

Samantha smiled, but only a little. She would have rather learned the answer to the plaid.

"Good luck with your puzzle pattern," said Lainey.

She headed across the street.

Samantha turned in the other direction and headed home.

CHAPTER TWENTY-TWO

IT WASN'T FAIR

*"The final score is Los Angeles, eighty-seven, Yankees . . .
zero.*

*"And with this incredible defeat, folks, the New York
Yankees are almost—"*

Nipper switched off the radio and sat down on the
edge of his bed.

Game one hundred forty-five was over. His Yankees
were in big, big trouble, and nobody was willing to help.

He flopped backward and stared up at the slowly ro-
tating blades of his ceiling fan.

"Two games left," he said softly. "Only two games
left."

Tomorrow his New York Yankees were scheduled to
play a doubleheader against Boston. His Yankees were

going to lose their final five games to the Red Sox. What could be worse?

The light in the center of the fan hurt his eyes, so he let his gaze drift down to a shelf above his desk. There, a dozen graphic novels lay in a stack.

"Someday *I'm* going to make a graphic novel about my life," Nipper sighed. "And when I do, I'm gonna call this part of the story 'It wasn't—'"

Something caught his eye. He sat up straight.

On the shelf, between the stack of graphic novels and a Mickey Mantle bobblehead, it had been sitting there all along.

He got up from the bed and went to take a closer look.

Nipper smiled.

He saw something . . . that could save his Yankees!

He walked over to his bedroom window and looked down. He spotted his sister, shuffling along the sidewalk. Her head drooped and she walked slowly, dragging her umbrella on the ground. She looked disappointed.

"Good," said Nipper. "My Yankees need me, and so does Sam."

He headed downstairs and waited for her to come back into the house.

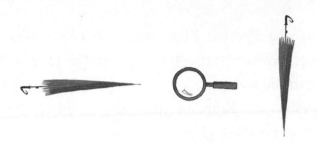

CHAPTER TWENTY-THREE

SAMANTHA, HEARS THE DEAL

As Samantha walked back to her house, she wrestled with a decision. *She could* head up to her room and write a gloomy poem in her journal *or . . .* she could flop onto the couch and power mope.

"Poem," she said grimly.

As she opened the front door, she had already started composing in her head:

> *Where, oh where did my uncle go?*
> *And why did he say "Watch out for the—*

"So!" Nipper called cheerfully the moment she stepped through the front door. "You want to figure out the *plaid pattern,* do you?"

Samantha ignored him. She wasn't interested in whatever ridiculous thing he was going to say. She headed to the stairs.

"I said . . . ," Nipper continued, "you'd like to see Uncle Paul's plaid. Right?"

"Is that really a question?" she replied.

"Well, today is a *lucky day*," said Nipper.

"Ugh," said Samantha. "Not another one of your lucky days. Don't you remember what happened last time you—"

"Not *my* lucky day," said Nipper. "Today is *your* lucky day."

Her brother bounced up and down on his toes. He seemed really excited.

"Don't you want to know the pattern in the plaid?" he asked.

"Okay," she said. "Right. I do."

"Perfect," he said, "because I've discovered the secret."

"Secret?" she asked.

"Yes," he said. "The secret to Uncle Paul's perplexing pants!"

Nipper stopped bouncing suddenly.

"Of course, before I share it with you," he said, pointing a finger at her, "you are going to help me do something . . . about this!"

He reached into his pocket and pulled out a shiny object.

"A coin?" asked Samantha.

Nipper looked at his hand. He was holding out a silver-colored object.

"Whoops," he said. "That's an old penny from Uncle Paul. Wrong pocket."

He tucked the silver-colored penny away, reached into a different pocket, and took out the green plastic scorpion ring.

Samantha sighed.

"And *why* exactly am I going to help you now?" she asked.

"Because," said Nipper, "I have the answer to your plaid puzzle."

He crossed his arms and flashed a big smile.

Samantha thought about it for a moment. Her brother seemed really excited and very certain that he knew something useful. He could be completely wrong, of course.

But she had reached a dead end.

"Okay," she told him. "What do I have to do?"

He handed her the fake plastic ring.

"You're going to help me steal the *real* scorpion ring from Missy Snoddgrass," he said.

"I don't really approve of stealing things," Samantha said.

"Are you kidding!" Nipper said. "Missy steals everything from me!"

He started marching around the room.

"She took my Yankees! She took my big blue diamond!" he shouted, waving his hands in the air. "Do you remember that gold, gem-covered egg sculpture that Uncle Paul gave me?"

Samantha nodded.

"She took that, too!" Nipper shouted. "And I used to have a trombone, and some cool round glasses, and a really old baseball card."

"I'm pretty sure you lost some of those all by yourself," Samantha said.

"It doesn't matter. And we're really trading, more than stealing," Nipper said.

He pointed out through the side window of the living room.

"If you can get us to Missy's back porch and help me get that ring, then I'll show you the *pattern* in the *plaid*."

Samantha looked out the window to their neighbor's house.

"All right," she said.

"Yes!" Nipper said, punching a fist happily at the air.

"Hold on," Samantha said.

She stuffed the plastic ring into her pocket.

"How exactly am I supposed to help get you the ring?" she asked.

"That's your job," said Nipper. "Do I have to figure out *everything*?"

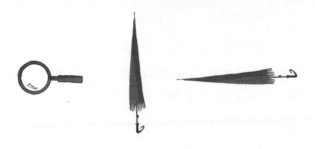

CHAPTER TWENTY-FOUR

OPERATION SNODDGRASS

"What's with the clipboard?" Nipper asked Samantha as they walked across their backyard.

"It's a prop," she answered. "I borrowed it from Mom. Now let me have your hand lens."

"Where's your umbrella?" he asked.

"I left it at home," said Samantha. "We won't need it."

Samantha hoped that was true. It had saved her life on more than one occasion. Finding secret passageways, fighting ninjas. But right now she just wanted to help her brother get his silly ring and then get back to finding her uncle.

Nipper took the magnifier from his pocket and handed it to her.

"Good," she said. "Let's go."

Together they hopped over the bushes and landed on the Snoddgrass driveway.

"See?" her brother told her. "It's a lot easier to get here this way, isn't it?"

"We went this way because we don't want anyone on the porch to see us," Samantha replied. "Just do as I say, and you'll get the ring."

"Sure, sure," said Nipper. "But that was a perfectly acceptable way to go between houses, am I right?"

Samantha didn't answer. She led him across the driveway. When they reached the side of the Snodd-grass house, just past the front porch, they crouched out of sight . . . and waited.

"If nobody touches my things . . . then nobody's bones will get broken!"

It was Missy, shouting back into the house as she stepped onto the front porch. The horrible little girl slammed the door behind her and marched down the steps. This was good. Samantha would be able to help her brother without having to worry about another Missy-versus-Nipper adventure.

They watched as Missy reached the sidewalk, turned, and disappeared in the direction of downtown Capitol Hill.

"You've memorized your script, right?" Samantha asked her brother.

"Yes," Nipper said. "Word for word."

"Fine," Samantha said. "Don't change anything, and I'll get us inside."

Nipper gave her a thumbs-up.

They walked around the front porch and up the steps. Nipper leaned flat against the house to the right of the door and out of sight.

Samantha rang the doorbell.

"Do you really think this will work, Sam?" Nipper whispered.

"Shhhh," she replied. "Just stick to the script."

The heavy door opened. A man and a woman stood behind the screen door, smiling.

Samantha was pretty sure they were Missy's parents. She'd encountered them the last time she'd gone to Missy's house. Of course, *every* time she went to this house, things were kind of strange. There always seemed to be something going on in this place that she couldn't quite figure out.

The man wore a chef's hat and a sparkling clean apron with the words BOSS-LEVEL GRILLER on it. In one hand, he held a long pair of metal tongs. A roasted hot dog dangled from them.

The woman wore a frilly apron. She cradled a blueberry pie. A toothpick stuck into the crust held a small blue ribbon with the words *FIRST PRIZE. NATIONAL BAKING COMPETITION*. The woman also had a blue ribbon pinned to her frock. That ribbon said *AWARD-WINNING BAKER OF NATIONAL BAKING COMPETITION. FIRST-PLACE WINNER.*

Yep, thought Samantha. *Kind of strange.*

Samantha could see Nipper out of the corner of her eye. He was leaning against the wall, with his eyes closed, sucking in long, deep breaths of the hot dog and blueberry pie scents wafting out of the home.

"*Stick to the script,*" she whispered.

He opened his eyes and nodded.

Samantha cleared her throat and leaned in to speak to the adults through the screen door.

"Cookie delivery," said Samantha.

"Cookies?" asked the man.

He pushed open the screen door and stepped forward. Nipper stood pinned between the door and the wall.

"Tell us about these cookies," he said.

The screen was pressed against Nipper's face, and the man waved his barbecue tongs in the air, dangling a hot dog two inches from Nipper's nose.

Samantha pretended to review information on the clipboard.

"It says . . . here," she said, "Missy ordered ten thousand boxes of cookies to help send me to detective train camp."

"Detective train camp?" asked the man.

"Ten . . . thousand . . . cookies?" asked the woman, stepping out of the house.

She looked past Samantha, out to the sidewalk, then up and down the street.

"Where?" she asked.

"I'm just the advance cookie delivery scout, ma'am," said Samantha politely. "Before the trucks can unload, I have to make sure the porch is safe."

"Safe?" the man and woman both asked at the same time.

"It has to support the weight of all the boxes," said Samantha.

She knelt down and pretended to inspect the floorboards through Nipper's hand lens.

"Take a close look at this porch," she said, gesturing with the clipboard for them to come join her.

The man let go of the door, and he and the woman both knelt down to peek at the wood through the lens of the magnifying glass. While they stared, Samantha waved to Nipper. He crept from behind the door and tiptoed into the house.

As soon as Nipper was out of sight, Samantha stood up.

"Excellent carpentry," she announced.

"That's good news," said the man.

Both of the strange adults got to their feet.

"And the cookies?" asked the woman.

"The truck should be here in five business days," said Samantha, pretending to read from the clipboard again. "Sometime between five a.m. and midnight."

The man and woman smiled, nodded, and walked back into the house.

Samantha watched the door swing shut behind them.

She hoped her brother would stick to the script.

CHAPTER TWENTY-FIVE

INSIDE OUT

Nipper stood in the center of the Snoddgrasses' foyer and waited. When the strange man and woman turned to reenter the house, he started jumping up and down. The two adults froze.

"I'm so glad I found you in time!" said Nipper.

"Wait. What? Who are you?" asked the man.

"In time for what?" said the woman.

"The cookies are ready!" Nipper said excitedly. "They're being unloaded in the park!"

"In the park?" asked the man, looking confused. "Why not in front of this house?"

"There were too many," said Nipper. "They're stacking them up in front of the art museum. You've got to go get them before it rains."

The man and the woman stared at him.

"You don't want to have to tell Missy that her cookies got soggy . . . and it was all your fault, do you?"

The two adults both gulped nervously.

"I bet that would make her really mad," he said. "And I mean really, really, really, really, really—"

They turned and ran onto the porch. The door slammed behind them. Nipper counted to ten. Then he opened the door again.

Samantha entered.

"Good job," she said, pulling the door closed behind her. "This mission is going exactly as planned."

"Not exactly," said Nipper.

"Why do you say that?" she asked.

"As long as you were tricking people, you *could* have tricked them into leaving us the hot dog," said Nipper longingly. "Or that blueberry pie."

"Hush," said Samantha. "And come on."

She left the foyer, with Nipper on her heels, and walked into a living room . . . sort of.

Dozens of fancy picture frames hung on the walls, but none of them held any pictures. They were all empty.

A large grandfather clock stood between two doorways, not ticking.

A framed needlepoint banner rested on a coffee table, with a message in needlepoint letters:

LOOSE LIPS SINK SHIPS

The floor was littered with knitting needles, crochet hooks, and balls of yarn. There were half a dozen rocking chairs, scattered about the room, plus a dog carrier. But there was no sign that any people had actually spent any time here. And there didn't seem to be any traces of a dog, either.

"I wonder what kind of 'living' takes place in this room," Samantha said to Nipper.

He shrugged.

"Let's just grab your bug ring and get out of here," Samantha said.

"Arachnid," Nipper said. "Which way is the back porch?"

Samantha looked around. Two doorways led out of the room. Through one opening, she saw a stove and a refrigerator. She could see a table and chairs through the other doorway.

"Let's split up," she said, pointing to the left. "You check out the kitchen."

"I'm on it," said Nipper.

She watched him head to the kitchen, but before he reached the doorway, he stopped and turned back to her.

"Sam?" he called.

"Yes," she replied, annoyed. "What now?"

"I just want to say thank you," he told her. "Thanks for helping. It means a lot to me."

Samantha smiled.

"And if my Yankees *were* here," he continued, "I'm sure they'd all want to thank you, too. And—"

"Hurry up," she said, cutting him off. "Just go and come back quickly!"

Nipper turned and disappeared into the kitchen.

She listened to his footsteps fade, and then she headed to the next room.

Samantha thought about this silly "mission." She and her brother were on yet another adventure, and once again, things were getting strange. As always, she and her brother seemed entangled in something bigger and weirder than they could ever have imagined.

She shook her head. She wasn't sure if she was thinking about sneaking into the Snoddgrass house just now, or about all the things that had happened this year to her and Nipper . . . and Dennis and her parents and Uncle Paul . . . and even to Buffy.

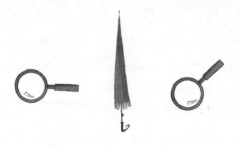

CHAPTER TWENTY-SIX

IRONY CHEF

Nipper stepped into the kitchen and looked around the room. A small table lined with spices in neat rows sat in the center, and along the back wall was an L-shaped counter with shelves above it filled with cans and boxes. A wood-paneled refrigerator hummed beside a shiny chrome oven. Colorful fruit hung in wire baskets.

Smelling the hot dogs and the pie at the front door had already made Nipper hungry. He was doing his best to *stick to the script,* but the delicious aroma of boss-level grilling and national-award-winning baking was a major distraction.

He took a deep breath, held it, and then let it out slowly.

He was there to get the ring.

To get the ring, he had to *find* the ring.

To find the ring, he had to find the back porch without finding a parrot.

To find . . .

. . . himself alone in a kitchen now, surrounded by food, was distracting!

"Time . . . out," he said, sounding a little like a sports announcer.

He was in a kitchen, all by himself. Snacks were everywhere. There was nothing to stop him, and there was nothing he wouldn't consider eating.

"Pickled crabmeat with oysters," said Nipper, reading words on a shiny copper can close to him on the counter.

Okay. Pickled crabmeat and oysters were some things he wouldn't consider eating. Probably. At the very least, they wouldn't be his first choice. He kept looking.

A thick paper bag with a clear plastic window rested on the counter. It was the kind of bag that usually had fresh-baked cookies inside. He read the label.

"Sea urchins?" said Nipper in surprise.

He shook his head and moved on to a row of big glass jars. One looked like it was full of powdered chocolate. The other looked like brown sugar.

"Hot chili . . . cumin," said Nipper, reading the labels on the jars.

He shook his head.

"Nope. Not today," he said to the jars, as if they could hear him.

Nipper crossed to the other side of the kitchen. He opened the refrigerator. Something flopped out onto the floor. It looked like the end of a fire hose. Nipper bent down to get a closer look. It was a long, gray, rubbery tube. One side was lined with rows of suction cups.

"A tentacle?" Nipper asked.

He rose to his feet and peered into the refrigerator. It was stuffed with a huge gray shape. Two basketball-sized spheres wobbled at eye level. They seemed to stare at Nipper like two big mysterious eyeballs.

They *were* eyeballs! A whole boiled giant squid filled the refrigerator!

"Ugh," said Nipper, shaking his head.

There was no way—no *way*—he would ever consider eating that! He was pretty sure.

He closed the refrigerator, irritated. Where were the tasty snacks? Where was the food that not-double-triple super-evil kids liked to eat?

A flickering light caught Nipper's attention. On the other side of the refrigerator, an old lightbulb dangled from the ceiling in a small walk-in pantry. The tiny room was lined with shelves, but they were empty . . . except for one shelf at Nipper's eye level. In the center of the wooden shelf stood a single box, about the size of a cereal box. It showed photos of graham crackers, marshmallows, and chocolate chips. Purple dots sparkled on the surfaces of the crackers. Letters made out of candy canes spelled out the words:

PEPPERMINT S'MORES COOKIES

Lower down on the box, words appeared in a yellow burst:

. . . with Pop Rocks!

"That's more like it," said Nipper.
He smiled and picked up the box and shook it.
It was empty.
"That figures," Nipper said.
Then, *snap!*
Somewhere inside the thick wooden shelf, there was a sound like a sprung mousetrap. Before he could say "Holy cow-a-bunga! What's happening?" the whole pantry, with Nipper inside it, dropped like a bag of rock salt.

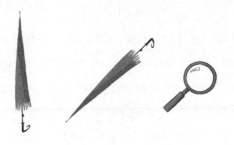

CHAPTER TWENTY-SEVEN

CRAZY MIXED-UP FILES

The pantry-elevator touched down. After such a sudden surprise drop, the landing was actually kind of gentle. Nipper stood, stunned, for a moment, facing the same shelves he'd been facing upstairs. Then he turned and peered out through the doorway.

A long corridor led away from the pantry-elevator. It was lined with metal cabinets. They looked a lot like the ones Nipper's dad had in his office, where he kept all his lightbulb notes, charts, and diagrams. Nipper counted ten cabinets on each side of the hallway.

He tried to read the labels on one of the cabinets, but the writing was small, and the light in the hallway wasn't very good. He reached for his hand lens, but then he remembered that Samantha had it.

The door at the other end of the hallway was half-open, and light streamed in from the space beyond. There was only one place to go, so he walked to the door and peeked through the opening.

The room seemed to be empty, so he pushed the door open and entered.

It was a tiny office. A desk, a floor lamp, and an old, wooden swivel chair were against the wall. Above the desk, two large, glossy photos were pinned to a bulletin board. Each one featured a smiling face. They were photos of Missy's parents.

Nipper leaned in for a closer look. "Craig Zilch," he read on the bottom of the photo of Missy's dad.

He scratched his head. That was odd. He'd expect the man's last name to be *Snoddgrass*. He inspected the second shiny photo.

"Lucinda Q. Blurglestein?" Nipper said.

He shook his head. Who *were* these people?

A folder on the desk was stuffed with papers. He opened it.

He gasped.

They looked like legal papers.

"My Yankees?" Nipper asked breathlessly.

Could he have found his player contracts and the deed to Yankee Stadium?

He took a closer look.

No. They weren't baseball player contracts. Nipper

hung his head sadly until something on the paper caught his eye.

"Model Parent Release Form," Nipper read. "Employment Agreement."

He scanned the first document. The page was filled with a ton of fine print that he wasn't interested in reading without his hand lens. He skipped to the bottom. In bigger print it said:

ROLE:
Jonathan Jacob Snoddgrass.

DESCRIPTION:
A friendly and mild-mannered father in his midforties. Winner of several World's Greatest Dad awards. Alert, confident, eager to please. Boss-level griller.

Nipper picked up a second contract:

ROLE:
Rebecca Jane Snoddgrass

DESCRIPTION:
A cheerful and energetic mother, president of the PTA. Kind, content, soft-spoken. Blueberry pie enthusiast. Frilly apron wearer.

Nipper shook his head and closed the folder. He

wasn't interested in contracts that didn't have anything to do with his Yankees.

He glanced sideways and noticed something on the wall to his right. An oil painting in a fancy gold frame.

The painting featured a boat—an old-fashioned sailing ship. A flag with a skull and eight bones sticking out of it flapped from the top of the main mast.

A pirate crew fired cannons and waved torches. Nipper counted ten . . . fifteen . . . twenty people on board.

Near the middle of the ship, a pirate captain waved his sword at some poor guy on a plank stretching out over the choppy water.

Nipper could swear the captain in the painting looked familiar. Nipper leaned forward to get a better look and gasped. It was Nathaniel, Buffy's one-legged pirate assistant! The man had attacked Nipper with a sword and probably would have killed him if a Komodo dragon hadn't saved Nipper!

He squinted to try to make out the person on the plank.

Wait . . . a . . . minute . . .

It was him!

"What? Huh? Who?" Nipper spluttered.

In the painting, Jeremy Bernard Spinner stood on the edge of the plank, about to plunge into the dark, choppy sea. He was wrapped in mustard-yellow-colored string, with his hands pinned to his sides. Sharks splashed in the water below, eagerly looking up at their next meal.

Nipper turned his back on the painting.

"How incredibly . . . awful," he said quietly, and shivered.

It really was awful. And alarming. And it probably was a big clue about really important things. He had to tell Sam!

Nipper left the room quickly.

"I bet this has something to do with the WIND," he said as he reached the pantry. "When I tell Sam all about this, she'll probably want to come back and explore . . ."

He spotted a box on one of the shelves.

"Peppermint s'mores cookies," he read from the box.

He picked it up and shook it.

The box was empty.

"It figures," said Nipper.

Snap!

ZOOM!

The pantry, with Nipper inside, shot upward.

CHAPTER TWENTY-EIGHT

REUNION

Samantha entered the dining room. It was huge! It covered more than half the ground level of the Snoddgrass house.

A long, wooden table stretched across the room. Samantha counted ten . . . fifteen . . . twenty chairs. At the far end, she saw a set of sliding glass doors. Yellow polka-dot drapes covered them. A blinking green dot flashed through the fabric.

"The back porch," said Samantha.

She heard a noise, and the house shook for a second.

"Nipper?" she asked.

Nothing. What was taking her brother so long?

Samantha spotted a big, framed map covering one wall. She went over to investigate.

"South Pacific Ocean," she said, reading a banner along the top of the frame.

Most of the map was blue, with islands scattered about.

In the upper left corner, she recognized Japan.

"*Domo arigato,*" said Samantha.

Uncle Paul had taught her how to say *Please, Thank you,* and *Where's the tallest building?* in Japanese. It was one of the eleven languages he'd taught her . . . before he'd started disappearing without telling her why, or where he was going.

Samantha's eye was drawn to a large mark, about halfway down the map, directly under Japan.

A red X covered a tiny island in the Pacific Ocean.

"Yap," said Samantha, reading the name beneath the spot on the map.

It sounded familiar, but Samantha couldn't remember where she had heard it before. Maybe she'd read about it somewhere.

"Yap?" she said again.

Samantha didn't think Uncle Paul had ever mentioned an island called Yap. Had she learned about it at school? Had she heard something about it in Buffy's ridiculous gold-plated New York apartment?

She heard another noise. The house shook again. Then she heard footsteps.

Samantha stood up straight and turned to see who was coming.

It was Nipper.

"I've been waiting here for ten minutes," she told him. "Where did you go?"

"It's not important," said Nipper, looking shaken up.

"The back porch is right here," Samantha said, gesturing to the glass doors.

The little green dot was blinking through the curtains, and Nipper smiled.

"Ready?" she asked.

Nipper nodded and crossed the room. He grabbed one of the handles on the sliding glass door.

"Good," she said, grabbing the other handle. "I've given up way too much of my afternoon for this goofy mission."

Together they pulled the doors apart.

"Let's get the bug ring and go," Samantha said as she pulled back the polka-dot drapes and stepped outside. "I need to head back and find Uncle—"

"Hello there, dumplings," said a high, sweet voice.

An elderly woman with blue-gray hair in curlers sat in a rocking chair on the porch. She wore a flowery bathrobe and sensible black leather shoes. She gazed at Samantha and Nipper through incredibly thick-lensed glasses and smiled warmly. As she rocked back and forth, she knitted a scarf using green knitting needles.

There was no sign of an emerald scorpion ring.

As the woman knitted and rocked, the light from an overhead lamp reflected off her knitting needles. Every few seconds, the tips of the needles flashed a green light.

Samantha glanced over at Nipper. He stood still, staring at the needles. He looked stunned.

"I get so few visitors these days," the woman said gently. "Come closer, sweet little boy, so I can pinch your cheeks."

The woman put down her knitting and reached out. Nipper stopped staring at the needles and stared at the woman's fingers. He took a step backward.

Samantha thought the woman's hands looked remarkably large and powerful. And hairy?

The woman sighed and gave up on pinching. She returned to her knitting. The green needles flashed several more times.

"I do hope you sweet little munchkins stay for a while," said the woman. "As soon as I finish this row, I'll brew some tea and open a box of peppermint s'mores cookies."

Samantha looked at Nipper. He stood frozen in place, watching the knitting needles.

"We're sorry to bother you, ma'am," said Samantha. "My brother and I were just passing through and . . ."

"Hello, Jeremy Bernard Spinner," said a voice.

Samantha spun around. Missy Snoddgrass stood in

the doorway, watching every move. Her yellow polka-dot blouse matched the drapes. The green emerald scorpion ring on her finger flashed.

"And sister," Missy added. "I see you've met my grandmother."

"Please," said the woman. "Call me *Nana*."

Nipper was silent. His eyes were locked on Missy's ring.

"I'm surprised to see you here, Jeremy," said Missy. "The Yankees have a double-header coming up. It could be their last game ever. I didn't think you'd want to miss closing day."

Her brother didn't say anything. His hands were balled into tight fists, his whole body shaking. He looked as if his head were about to explode.

Samantha knew it was time to step in and help.

"Hey, Missy," she called. "Can I show you what our uncle gave us?"

"Huh?" Missy grunted.

Samantha pulled the mitten from her back pocket, unrolled it, and held it out for Missy to inspect.

"This seems like an ordinary mitten, I know," Samantha told Missy. "But it gives you *extra protection*. Let me show you."

Missy looked at her suspiciously. Then, slowly, she stuck out her open hand.

Using both hands, Samantha slid the mitten over Missy's fingers and pushed until it touched her wrist.

Missy stared at the mitten on her hand.

"Well?" asked Samantha.

"Well what?" Missy replied, still staring at the mitten.

Nipper watched Missy carefully. He didn't move or say anything.

Samantha let out a big, dramatic sigh.

"Well . . . I guess that's not a good look for you," she said.

Missy nodded, leaving her hand out.

Samantha pulled the mitten off, rolled it up, and stuffed it into her back pocket again. As she did, she pulled out the fake plastic ring that Nipper had given her earlier.

Missy continued staring at her open hand.

"Whoopsy," said Samantha, holding up the second ring. "You don't want to lose this."

Missy snatched the ring and slipped it onto her finger.

Samantha glanced at Nipper. He still hadn't moved, but his eyes had grown wider. She thought she could make out a faint smile on his lips.

"Are . . . you going to stay for tea and cookies?" Nanna asked sweetly.

Samantha shook her head. "Thanks," she said. "But we were just leaving. Come on, Nipper."

"Exit through the porch, please," said Missy quickly, pointing to her backyard.

Nipper suddenly looked alarmed.

"Don't worry," Missy told him. "I'll make sure my parrot doesn't bother you."

She opened the screen door on the back of the porch with one hand and gestured with the other.

"For at least fifteen seconds," she added. "Now go!"

CHAPTER TWENTY-NINE

KNIT WITS

"You can take off the wig now," said Missy Snoddgrass. "They're gone."

"Arrrrrr . . . you sure?" asked Nathaniel.

"Yes," she answered. "I just watched them hop over the bushes together."

"Good," he said, yanking from his head the frizzy hairpiece loaded with curlers. "These fake locks are as itchy as barnacle bloomers."

The pirate tossed the blue-gray wig across the porch. Curlers clattered on the wood flooring. He kicked off one of his shoes, leaned back in the rocking chair, and returned to his knitting.

Missy sniffed the air twice.

"Is that really necessary?" she asked. "Your foot smells terrible."

"If you had bought me a bigger shoe, I wouldn't be in such a hurry to take it off," Nathaniel answered.

"Sorry," said Missy. "All the stores in the Pacific Northwest are sold out of size-ten ladies' shoes . . . ever since *Shoe Day*."

Missy lifted her hand and stared at the ring on her finger. She smiled as she watched the green scorpion blink. Then she pulled it off and dropped it onto the floor.

Crunch!

She stepped on it.

"What in blue blazes did you do that for?" asked the pirate, looking up from his knitting. "That bauble looked priceless."

"That *bauble* was a cheap plastic ring with a battery inside," said Missy.

"Aye . . . sea," said Nathaniel.

He went back to his knitting.

Missy closed her eyes and listened to the clicking sounds of the pirate's needles for a while. When she opened her eyes, she squinted through the screen wall of the porch. She studied the apartment above the Spinners' garage . . . and grinned.

"Put down the knitting needles," she said, turning

to face Nathaniel again. "I've got an important new assignment for you."

The pirate stopped knitting. He tilted his head down and looked at Missy over the top of his thick lenses.

"I need you to travel somewhere for me," she told him.

"Arrrrr-gentina?" asked Nathaniel. "Aye-celand? Myan-marrrrr?"

"No," said Missy. "Michigan."

"Michigan," Nathaniel repeated. "Are you sending me to Port Huron? Bay City? Ann Arrrrrrr-bor?"

Missy shook her head. She held up her hand so Nathaniel could see the mitten shape of Michigan.

"Go to Detroit," she said.

She pointed to a spot at the base of her thumb.

"Stay hidden until you find Paul Spinner."

Camouflage

Many animals have fur or skin with a combination of patterns and colors to help them hide or impersonate other things. This is called *camouflage*.

A leopard's spots help it disappear into the grass and trees. A saturniid moth imitates the face of an owl to scare other animals away.

People use camouflage, too. Soldiers wear camouflage uniforms to avoid being seen. Navies have even painted wild patterns on their battleships to make them difficult

to identify. A chameleon can alter its skin color to blend in
with its surroundings.

* * *

The WIND is highly skilled in the art of camouflage, and
they do it—with yarn!

Their pirate ship is covered with knitted blankets, so it
looks like a garage in someone's backyard. The entrance
to their secret underground headquarters is disguised as
a big grandfather clock in someone's living room. Members of the organization can even camouflage themselves
by wearing knitted clothing that blends in around statues,
paintings, and other works of art.

Watch out for the camouflage, so you can watch out
for the WIND!

CHAPTER THIRTY

MITTEN ACCOMPLISHED

"Pretty sneaky, Sam," said Nipper, inspecting the scorpion ring.

Samantha walked ahead of her brother as they crossed through their backyard. She wore a satisfied smile on her face.

"I'm going to destroy this thing," said Nipper. "I'm going to put an end to this evil curse."

Samantha stopped walking and turned around. Nipper was holding the ring right over his ring finger. He seemed to be trying really hard to stop himself from putting it on.

"Come on, Nipper," she said. "You know evil magical curses aren't real, don't you?"

"No . . . I mean, yes. I don't . . . ," he answered. "I mean no, I do, Sam."

She shook her head. "I'm getting tired of saying it," she told him. "But you're ridiculous . . . and annoying . . . and there's no such thing as a magical cursed ring."

"Oh yeah?" asked Nipper. "Then how do you explain the fact that it blinks?"

He held out his open palm with the scorpion ring in the center. She studied it for a second.

"Watch," she answered, taking it from him.

She held up the ring and slowly tilted it. The scorpion blinked. Then she rotated her hand slightly. The ring caught the light again and it flashed green once more.

"See?" she told him. "It just reflects light at different angles."

Nipper watched as she kept turning her hand. The ring flashed a few more times.

"Okay, Sam," he said. "Then how do you explain all the bumps and trips and stumbles that happened to me when I wore it?"

"Are your shoelaces tied?" she asked.

"Well . . . no," he replied, glancing down at his feet.

"Do you ever watch where you're going?" she asked. "Or look at what you're about to step on?"

"Not really," Nipper answered.

"Do you pay attention to your surroundings?" she continued. "Do you take a closer look at things before you touch or tap or poke or taste—"

"Okay, okay," he said, snatching the ring back from her. "Just forget about it."

They had reached the side of their house. Samantha stopped on the porch. She didn't open the door.

"I'm not forgetting *everything*," she said.

"What do you mean?" asked Nipper.

"I'm not forgetting what you promised," she said. "You said that if I helped you, you'd tell me the secret of the plaid."

"Oh yeah. You're right," said Nipper. "I almost forgot."

He shoved the ring into his pocket.

"Come with me," he said. "It'll bring back some memories."

Samantha followed her brother into the house and up to his bedroom, where she had a lot of good memories. . . . And some others she would gladly forget.

CHAPTER THIRTY-ONE

PLAID MOON RISING

Samantha sat down on the edge of Nipper's bed. Her brother stood next to his desk. He looked very excited to tell her something.

"All right," she said. "This had better be good."

Nipper took a deep breath.

"Do you remember last year, Sam?" he asked.

"Most of it," she answered.

"No, no," said Nipper, shaking his head. "Listen."

He took another deep breath.

"Do you remember when we all went to Pacific Pandemonium last year?" he asked.

"How could I forget?" Samantha replied.

Last year, the whole Spinner family, including Uncle Paul, had visited Pacific Pandemonium Amusement

Park, near Spokane, Washington. Her brother had ridden the Holy Cow-a-Bunga roller coaster thirteen times, until he'd thrown up and they'd all had to leave the amusement park early. Samantha wasn't going to forget about it for a long, long time.

"I remember how gross it was," she said. "And I remember having to leave before I got to ride It's a Big Little World, which is my favorite ride."

"That's really more of a musical theater show than a ride," said Nipper. "And it's for babies."

"So what?" Samantha snapped. "And why are we talking about this anyway?"

"Waitaminute, waitaminute, waitaminute," said Nipper. "Do you remember the last thing we did before we got into the car to go home?"

Samantha tried to remember. The whole experience had been exceptionally gross. What special detail could her brother be talking about?

"Okay, I'll tell you," said Nipper.

He reached over to the top of his desk, grabbed something, and held it behind his back.

"We got inside a photo booth together," said Nipper. "You, me, and Uncle Paul."

Samantha thought about it for a moment. She remembered that photo booth.

"Yes, we did!" she answered, slowly getting excited, too.

The hair on the back of her neck stood up. Could it be?

"Yes!" Nipper shouted. "And we paid eight dollars and ninety-nine cents . . . for this!"

He held out a glossy strip with four square black-and-white photos.

Samantha leaned forward and stared.

The top photo showed the three of them—Samantha, Nipper, and Uncle Paul—squeezed together on a bench inside a photo booth. In the photo, her brother and her uncle were smiling, but she looked mad. Samantha remembered being mad because they were leaving the park before she could go on the It's a Big Little World ride.

In the second photo, Nipper looked queasy. Samantha and Uncle Paul were watching him, worried that he was going to be sick again.

In the third photo, Nipper's eyes were closed, and he was covering his mouth with both hands. Samantha and her uncle were only half in the picture. They were scrambling to get up and out of the photo booth very, very quickly.

In the bottom photo, the camera had gone off just as Uncle Paul had left the booth. His rear end must have been right in front of the camera. The picture was a rectangle . . . of plaid!

"Thanks!" Samantha shouted, snatching the photo strip from Nipper.

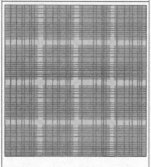

She raced out of her brother's room, across the hall, and straight into her bedroom. Her purple glasses sat on her desk, ready for her to inspect the pattern in the plaid.

CHAPTER THIRTY-TWO

LENS ME A HAND

Samantha sat down at her desk. Then she put on the purple glasses, held up the photo strip, and stared at the plaid rectangle at the bottom.

Nothing.

She took them off, rubbed the glasses against her sleeve to clean the lenses, and put them on again.

She stared. And stared. And . . . nothing.

"Ugh," she said. "Of course."

Of course it didn't work. Uncle Paul hadn't left a message in super-secret ink on Nipper's souvenir photo. It was just a picture . . . taken by accident . . . of his butt.

Samantha felt dumb . . . and frustrated . . . and was staring at a butt.

This was a total waste of time. . . . *Again.*

She took the glasses back off and let out a heavy sigh. She set down the photo and glasses and leaned forward.

Thump.

She let her head hit the top of her desk.

"Everything okay?" Mr. Spinner asked.

Samantha lifted her head and turned to see her father in the doorway. He looked worried.

"No, Dad," she told him. "Everything is *not* okay."

She held up the photo strip.

"The pattern is in the plaid," she said quietly. "And I'm . . . lost."

"Wait," he said, stepping into the room. "One minute."

He took the photo strip from her and stared at it.

Samantha could tell he was looking at each photo, one by one, starting at the top.

She knew when he reached the third photo, because he chuckled. He was definitely looking at Nipper.

Then her father reached the photo at the bottom, and he squinted.

His lips moved silently. Then, still squinting at the picture, he said, "One, one, two, three . . ."

Her father was counting. Samantha started getting excited. Had he found a clue?

"Five, eight . . . ," he continued.

Samantha held her breath.

"It's the Fibonacci sequence," said Mr. Spinner.

"The Fib-o-what?" she asked.

"It's a famous math pattern," he answered. "It's hidden in the pattern in this photo."

Her father put the photo strip on the desk in front of her and tapped one of the squares in the plaid.

"If you count the groups of stripes that run up and down, you get one, one, two, three," said Mr. Spinner.

Samantha nodded at him, then went back to looking at the photo.

"Now count the groups of stripes that go from side to side," he told her.

Samantha studied the square carefully.

"Five . . . eight," she replied.

"Exactly," said her father. "That's the Fibonacci sequence. Every number is the sum of the two numbers before it. You start with two ones to make the number two. Then you add two and—"

"Wait," said Samantha, standing up quickly.

She pushed her chair back under her desk.

"Come with me and explain it. I want to write it all in my journal."

He smiled and nodded, and together they headed downstairs to the kitchen.

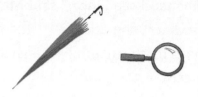

CHAPTER THIRTY-THREE

THE GOOD, THE PLAID, AND THE . . . PUGLY?

"It's pronounced 'fih-buh-nah-chee,'" Mr. Spinner told Samantha as they entered the kitchen. "It's one of the most famous number patterns in the world."

He took a pencil and a sheet of paper from a drawer. Then he sat down at the table. He waved for Samantha to join him.

"Each number is the sum of the two numbers right before it," he said, as he wrote on the paper:

1, 1, 2, 3, 5, 8, 13, 21 . . .

"One plus one is two. One plus two is three. Two plus three is five," he said. "Get it?"

"I think so," said Samantha.

She opened her journal to the page where she had started copying the number grid from the secret wall in the Detroit Institute of Arts.

"Here's a wall with buttons," she said. "Do you think that I can use the Fibonacci sequence to open it and find the SNOW?"

"The who?" Mr. Spinner replied.

"The mathematicians," said Samantha. "You know, the ones that *you* gave Uncle Paul away to, the moment I turned my back for *two minutes*. Thanks a lot."

"It was Paul's idea to go with them, Samantha," her father said. "He did it to save Nipper, by going in his place."

He watched her think about it for a moment.

"Or . . . maybe he planned it all," said Mr. Spinner. "So you would follow him to someplace special."

Samantha was already busy circling all the numbers on the grid that fit the sequence.

"Nipper and I took the *kogelbaan* to Detroit, and I found a hidden entrance to a salt mine filled with treasures," she said. "We popped out of a secret door under a statue, but then they lost us in the museum using some kind of mysterious—"

She stopped circling and looked up.

Samantha had completely forgotten that her father didn't know all of Uncle Paul's secrets . . . or any of *her* super secrets!

What had she just done?

She looked at him nervously. He smiled, just as he normally did. He didn't seem very surprised to hear any of this.

"I know that you and your uncle travel around using secret transportation systems, Samantha," he said.

"You do?" she asked, surprised.

Her father nodded.

"When we went searching for your brother, Paul showed me the magtrain," he said.

He looked back down at the drawing.

"And the slidewalk," he added.

He started circling some of the numbers with his pencil.

"I know you wanted some of this to be secret," he said. "And I could tell you wanted to have something special, just between you and Uncle Paul."

"What about Mom?" Samantha asked.

"I think . . . your mother's the only one left in this family who doesn't know about the super secrets," he said.

Mr. Spinner glanced through the doorway toward the living room, where Dr. Spinner sat on the sofa. He watched her thoughtfully.

"There's a high probability that that's not going to last much longer," he said. "Eighty-nine . . ."

Samantha watched him finish circling the numbers.

"One hundred forty-four," he said, and put down his pencil.

"Are you guys talking about my Yankees?" Nipper asked, appearing in the kitchen doorway. "There's only two games left until they lose one hundred forty-seven and—"

"Your time limit is exceeded," said Samantha. "And we're not talking about baseball. We're figuring out how to get to the SNOW."

Nipper walked over to the table and stared down at their work.

"I'm teaching your sister about the Fibonacci sequence," said Mr. Spinner.

Nipper eyed the sketch. He frowned.

"This is like a foreign language lesson with Uncle Paul," said Samantha.

"No," said Nipper, backing away from the table. "This is a *math* lesson."

Her brother moved to the far side of the kitchen and sat down on the floor next to Dennis. The pug started licking his fingers.

"*Math class is tough,*" said Nipper. "*Math class is tough.*"

"What put that notion into your head, Son?" asked Mr. Spinner.

"Uncle Paul gave me a talking doll once," he answered. "I listened to it a lot . . . until a raccoon snatched it and ran away."

Samantha watched Dennis again. He had finished with Nipper's fingers and was licking furiously at her brother's wrist.

Samantha shook her head. The pug was licking salt.

"You haven't washed at all since we've been back?" she asked. "I took a shower the minute we got home. You are exceptionally—"

"*Math class is tough,*" Nipper repeated.

"Okay, Samantha," said Mr. Spinner.

He tapped on the sketch to get her attention.

"These are all the numbers. Is this what you wanted to find?"

She hoped it was! She closed her journal and stood up from the table.

"I wonder what other math challenges these SNOW people have created," he added.

Samantha could tell that her father was hoping to come with her, but she wasn't so sure he'd be a good traveling companion. She didn't think he cared about her nearly half as much as he cared about lightbulbs.

Then she looked at Nipper again. Dennis was licking under his sleeve. Nipper had a goofy this-tickles-and-I'm-trying-not-to-giggle expression. It was gross.

"If there are more puzzles like this, I could help you with the math," said Mr. Spinner. "And, of course, I'm good with lightbulb emergencies, too."

"I know, Dad," she replied. "But I'm not really expecting any lightbulb—"

"That's a great idea!" her brother shouted, interrupting.

He stood up and brushed some salt dust from his knees.

"I have a plan to stay home and get clean," he added.

"Really? Since when?" Samantha asked.

"Bath not math!" Nipper began chanting, and he raised a fist in the air. "Bath not math!"

She didn't believe her brother would actually go through with it and take a bath, but this was a new kind of super-annoying behavior, and it was very effective.

"Bath not math!" Nipper repeated.

"Fine," said Samantha. "You stay here. Dad, come help find Uncle Paul."

"This will be illuminating," Mr. Spinner said cheerfully.

Samantha sighed. She wasn't sure that her father was going to be more helpful or less annoying than her brother.

"You should bring Dennis with you, too," said Nipper.

Samantha looked down at the pug. She couldn't see

his face anymore. His cone was pressed against Nipper's leg. She heard the soft sandpaper sound of dog tongue on salty blue jeans.

"Why do you think I should bring Dennis?" Samantha asked.

"Haven't you noticed, Sam?" replied Nipper. "He saves us all the time."

He reached down and patted the dog's plastic cone.

"Whenever we're in big trouble, Dennis has a moment of greatness," said Nipper. "I think he saves us because we're his friends."

Dennis began licking Nipper's knuckles.

"Or maybe he's just looking for snacks and . . . Heehee! Stop that!" Nipper laughed.

Samantha thought about it. He had a point, but she didn't want to have to keep track of fathers, uncles, mathematicians, *and* pugs.

"He's safer here with you and Mom," she said.

Her father pushed his chair away from the table and stood up.

"Ready to solve this mystery?" he asked.

"Almost," said Samantha. "There's something I need to get first."

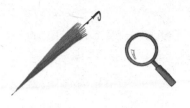

CHAPTER THIRTY-FOUR

HEAD OUT

Samantha and her father stood outside their garage in the backyard.

"Hold these for me," she said, handing him her red umbrella and Nipper's hand lens.

She grasped the garage door handle and yanked it upward, and the door rolled up and out of sight.

The space inside was filled with huge cardboard boxes, neatly labeled and stacked to the ceiling. In between were pinball machines, exercise equipment, and other loose items.

"I remember that popcorn popper," said Mr. Spinner.

Samantha remembered it, too. When she and Nipper had stayed with Buffy in New York, her sister had made them sleep in bare stables on piles of shredded newspaper. Her parents had gotten to stay in a deluxe guest suite filled with arcade machines, massage chairs, and an old-fashioned popcorn popper.

Samantha searched until she located a box marked FASHION DISASTER. She tore off the tape and opened the top. Inside were a pair of greenish-gray rubber boots, a deck of Word Whammy! cards, a stack of travel brochures, and a black top hat.

"Here," she told her father, picking up the hat and holding it out to him. "I need you to wear this."

"A stovepipe topper?" he asked. "Why?"

"It's too big for me, Dad," she answered. "See?"

Samantha put the hat on her head. It slid down over her eyes and stopped at her nose. She took it off and pointed it away from both of them, holding the rim with both hands. She squeezed the rim of the top hat.

Zing-zing!

A red leather boxing glove shot out from the top of the hat on the end of a spring, then zipped back inside.

"This belonged to one of those clowns in the SUN," she told him. "We might need it . . . for extra protection."

"Sure," said her father, taking it from her.

He handed back the umbrella and magnifier and adjusted the top hat on his head.

Samantha smiled. Buffy would not be happy to see this.

"Great," she told him. "We'll start by heading downtown to the *kogelbaan*."

"Whatever that is, I'm ready," said her father.

"Then we'll ride through the salt mine and come out of *The Thinker*," she said.

"I'm all for intellectual pursuits," he replied.

"It's a statue, Dad," said Samantha.

He nodded.

"I'll show you the monocycle pit along the way," she told him. "But I don't want to waste too much time before we go to the museum."

"Good," said Mr. Spinner. "And I'll be there to keep track of any mathematical details . . . or illumination issues."

He helped Samantha close the garage door, and then they walked down the driveway and headed downtown.

Along the way, they discussed magtrain mailboxes and slidewalk fire hydrants. She told him about the *kogelbaan* and the daredevils of the CLOUD, and how the SUN clowns had chased them from Mali to Seattle to Buffy's theater in New York.

It felt weird traveling with her father instead of Nipper. But now she felt ready for any trouble the SNOW might throw her way.

"Your brother might have had a point," Mr. Spinner said as they approached the car wash.

"What?" Samantha asked. "Bath not math?"

"No," he answered. "It might have been a good idea to bring Dennis."

The Fibonacci Sequence

The Fibonacci sequence is a famous mathematical pattern. To find the next number in the sequence, add the previous two numbers together.

It is named after the Italian mathematician Leonardo Pisano Bonacci, who lived in Italy from 1170 to 1250. His nickname was *Fibonacci*, which meant "son of Bonacci."

The Fibonacci sequence is a fun way to explore patterns in math. It can also be used to explore patterns in nature.

Nautilus shells, pine cone points, some cacti, and many other living things grow with patterns that match the Fibonacci sequence.

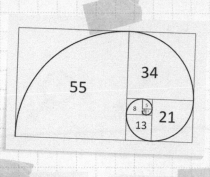

55 34

8 5
13 21

* * *

Find the secret number wall hidden in the Detroit Institute of Arts. Press all the buttons that have numbers that are part of the Fibonacci sequence. When you've made all the correct numbers light up, the whole wall will slide open.

You'll be able to enter the headquarters of the SNOW.

CHAPTER THIRTY-FIVE

APPLICATION

"Hi, Mom," said Nipper as he stomped into the living room.

His mom sat on the sofa, holding a book open. The cover said, *Discover Your Inner Pangolin*. She watched him carefully.

"Whatcha doing?" he asked.

"Reading," she said. "And keeping an eye on you."

He saw her glance over at the big box of markers on top of the bookshelf. Then she looked at the vacuum cleaner on the floor beside it.

"The last time you were here without your sister, you tried to launch those markers using—"

"I don't have any time for experiments," he interrupted. "Because I have some questions for you to answer."

His mom looked him up and down. She seemed to be inspecting his clothes.

"I thought I heard you chanting about taking a bath," she said.

He slapped his chest with one hand. A cloud of salty dust rose from his shirt.

"I took a dust bath," he said. "You know. Like a chinchilla."

His mom coughed softly and fanned the air with her book.

"Speaking of rodents," Nipper said quickly, "did you know there are rodents with poop shaped like cubes?"

"Of course," she answered. "Wombats."

Nipper glanced down at the note cards he'd brought with him, and then looked up at his mom.

"Right," he said. "And did you know that a chameleon's tongue can be three feet long?"

"I do," said his mother. "But it would have to be a large species, like the Malagasy giant chameleon."

Nipper began to pace back and forth in front of the couch.

"You really know a lot of facts, Mom," he said.

"I know a lot of rodent and lizard facts," she said. "I'm a veterinarian, and that's my specialty. Why are you suddenly so interested in rodents and lizards?"

Nipper stopped in front of the couch.

"I've been thinking," he said. "You're always asking

me and Dad about WRUF, the Worldwide Reciters of Useless Facts."

"Well . . . ," she said. "The two of you do always seem to be spouting strange bits of information, and I—"

"It's not fair to leave you out," Nipper interrupted. "I mean, why should the Spinner boys have all the fun?"

" 'Spinner boys'?" she asked. "Does that include Dennis and your uncle?"

"I think *you* have what it takes, Mom," Nipper continued. "I mean . . . maybe."

He scratched his chin thoughtfully.

"Not everyone is qualified, though," he added.

Nipper pulled several pages of paper from his back pocket.

"A lot of people *think* they're experts on things like science or nature," he said, waving the papers at her. "This application is meant to screen out people who don't know as much as they think they do."

"Let me see that," said Dr. Spinner taking the papers quickly.

Nipper watched her read through the first page of the application. He handed her a pencil.

"Biggest fish?" she read out loud. "That's easy. Blue whale."

Nipper shook his head.

"Wait," she said quickly. "A whale's not a fish. It's a mammal. The biggest fish is . . . some kind of a shark."

"Whale shark," said Nipper.

"Yes. I knew that," said Mrs. Spinner.

She looked at him. Then looked over to the door.

"Listen," she told him. "I could do a lot better on this if I had no distractions."

"Fine with me, Mom," said Nipper. "I'll go make myself useful. Maybe I'll check on Dennis."

"Dentist? No," said his mother. "A tooth and jaw expert is an *orthodontist.*"

Nipper could tell she was on page two of the application.

He grabbed his backpack from the floor and headed up to his room.

CHAPTER THIRTY-SIX

TRAVELING LIGHT

Nipper walked around his bedroom, collecting things.

He picked up an old baseball glove that Uncle Paul had given him and put it into his backpack.

"Extra protection," he said.

Nipper found an old deck of playing cards and an old board game.

"Entertainment," he said, stuffing them into the backpack, too.

He looked over at his desk and saw a bobblehead. It was Mickey Mantle, one of the greatest New York Yankees of all time. He stuffed that into the back-pack, for good luck. Then he headed back down-stairs.

He passed his mom in the living room.

She was still on the couch, reading through the WRUF application.

"The Nile?" he heard her say to herself. "I could have sworn the Amazon was the longest river in the world."

Nipper didn't say anything to her. He headed around the corner to his dad's office. He went inside and spotted a headlamp hanging from a hook by the door. He took it down and flipped a switch, and the light came on.

"Illumination," said Nipper, stowing the headlamp in his backpack.

He spotted an empty tote bag hanging on the hook. It had the letters EPE printed on it.

The Exotic Pet Expo was the pet convention where Mr. Spinner had bought Dennis his Blinky Barker automatic light-up dog collar a few months ago.

"That reminds me," said Nipper.

He went to his dad's desk, opened the drawer, and took out one of the experimental high-power lightbulbs Mr. Spinner often brought home from work.

"Extra illumination," said Nipper. "Just in case."

He rolled up the tote bag and stuffed it into his backpack, too. Then he slipped the lightbulb into his pocket, left the office, and headed to the kitchen.

"Wruf!" Dennis barked when he saw Nipper coming.

Nipper opened a cabinet and grabbed a box of granola bars. He took one out and waved it at Dennis as he stuffed the box into his pack.

"Wruf!" the dog barked excitedly.

"Yes," said Nipper. "This is for you."

He dropped the bar onto the floor.

Dennis trotted over to the bar and sniffed it happily. He opened his mouth and moved toward the bar. Then he stopped and looked up at Nipper suspiciously.

"No, old pal," said Nipper. "This isn't a trick."

Nipper reached out to pat the pug on his head, but Dennis pulled back. Nipper patted the rim of his plastic cone.

He was pretty sure he knew what Dennis was thinking. They were best friends, but a big part of their relationship revolved around fighting each other over crackers, waffles, and granola bars.

"Yes, yes. It's a present," Nipper reassured him.

While Dennis munched away, Nipper reached for the plastic Blinky Barker collar around the dog's neck. He removed the lightbulb, set it on the kitchen counter, and replaced it with the one he'd taken from his father's office.

He peeked through the doorway into the living room. His mother was busy studying the WRUF application. Good. While she was distracted, it gave him time to sneak out and set things right.

Nipper patted the dog one more time on his cone. Then he opened the back door.

"Come on," he said. "We've got a team to save."

CHAPTER THIRTY-SEVEN

NIPPER SPINNER AND THE SUPER PLAN

Four months ago, Nipper's uncle had disappeared for the first time. Uncle Paul had left some money to Nipper's sister Buffy, and an umbrella to his sister Sam. But Nipper had gotten the most special, most precious gift of all: the New York Yankees.

And then . . . he *lost* them!

While he was showing off the contracts to his neighbor Missy Snoddgrass, she asked him for a trade. He didn't pay attention and agreed to swap his Yankees for an old hand lens. By the time he realized his mistake, it was too late. His Yankees were gone, and every time he tried to get them back, he failed miserably.

But that was only half of the horrible story.

After Nipper traveled with Sam to a secret tomb in

Edfu, Egypt, he brought back an emerald scorpion ring. His sister didn't believe in evil magical curses, but she was completely wrong about a lot of things. The ring had an ancient Egyptian curse.

Nipper gave it to Missy as a "present," to get revenge on her for stealing his Yankees . . . and it backfired completely. Missy was so evil that the curse had no effect on her. His Yankees, however, began to lose, and lose and lose.

Now they were on the edge of disaster, just one game away from doom. It was time to set things right.

Nipper Spinner had a plan.

Standing beside Dennis at the corner of Thirteenth Avenue and Aloha, he opened and closed the metal mailbox drawer three times. The steel chamber rose from the street. When the staircase locked into place, Nipper led Dennis down the stairs with him into the magtrain station. Minutes later, they were on the high-speed magnetic train cruising toward Edfu, Egypt.

As he sat in the center seat of the magtrain, racing along at ten thousand miles per hour, Nipper took the emerald scorpion ring from his pocket and studied it. The rear six legs of the figurine curved to form the hole, waiting for an unlucky finger to go through it. The tiny green pincers twinkled with the passing light of the tunnel.

"Wruf! Wruf!" Dennis barked from the train bench behind him.

"Don't worry, pal," Nipper replied. "I'm not going to put this on again. It's evil . . . and dangerous . . . and a destroyer of Major League Baseball teams."

Samantha said the curse was all in his mind, and that his Yankees were just having a bad season. But she was too distracted about their missing uncle to understand the record-breaking sports tragedy. It was exactly the kind of thing that comes from ancient curses. The team was facing ultimate doom, and it would be all his fault.

It was up to Nipper Spinner to save his team . . . and he had a plan.

"Yankees are the best. The best. The best," Nipper chanted quietly as the magtrain motors hummed.

Dennis stared at him, his ears flapping in the breeze from the tunnel.

Nipper set the ring beside him on the seat and reached over his shoulder. He pulled the deck of old playing cards from a side pocket of his backpack.

"I've got twenty minutes to kill," he said. "I might as well have some fun and . . ."

Just as he fanned the cards out on the dashboard of the train, a sudden gust of air rushed over the train's windshield and swept the cards away. They fluttered into the air like a swarm of mad butterflies, and he watched them disappear into the tunnel behind him.

He looked down at the ring.

"See that," he said to Dennis. "Just being close to the ring might have made that happen."

He unzipped the top of his backpack and looked at the old board game.

"Nah," said Nipper. "It takes too long to set up that game."

He closed his pack and faced forward as the wind whipped at his hair. It felt odd to be headed back to Edfu, Egypt, without Samantha. The last time he'd been there, she'd saved him from sliding into a horrible bottomless pit. She'd also tried to stop him from taking the evil scorpion ring home with him. He should have listened, but that was ancient history.

The train began to slow. He shoved the ring back into his pocket and peeked into the backpack again.

"Headlamp . . . check," he said. "Granola bars . . . check."

"Wruf! Wruf!" barked Dennis, causing his collar light to turn on and off quickly.

"Dog . . . check," said Nipper.

He patted the baseball bat on one side of the backpack, held in place by bungee cords. "Check."

He had lights, a snack, a dog, and extra protection. He was ready. He would travel to the deepest, creepiest part of the tomb beneath the Temple of Horus. There he'd toss the evil ring into the bottomless pit. The emerald scorpion would be gone forever, and the curse would be lifted from his Yankees.

The magtrain came to a stop. Nipper slung the backpack over his shoulder, hopped onto the Edfu station platform, and headed up the ramp.

He smiled and looked back to make sure Dennis was following him.

"Come on, pal," he said. "This is going to be—"

"Wruf!" barked Dennis.

"Nah," said Nipper, shielding his eyes from the dog collar's light. "This'll be easy."

CHAPTER THIRTY-EIGHT

TEAM SPIRIT

Nipper climbed out of the magtrain. He passed through a hallway lined with paintings of the Egyptian god Horus. The walls were covered with tiled mosaics of ancient buildings and gods. It was pretty cool, but he didn't stop to look at anything. He'd been there before, and right now he was in a hurry. His Yankees were probably getting near the end of the first game of their doubleheader. They were probably losing game number one hundred forty-six.

Nipper arrived at a small room with a ladder in the center rising up to a hole in the ceiling.

He reached up to grasp the ladder and began to climb. After two rungs, he stopped and looked back down. Dennis sat looking up at him.

"Wruf!" Dennis barked.

Nipper looked back down. The pug looked up at him.

"Whoops," said Nipper, hopping to the ground. "I almost forgot."

He reached into his backpack, took out the tote bag, and unrolled it.

"A pug tote," said Nipper, holding the bag open against the floor. "Hop in."

Dennis sniffed the bag. He didn't seem interested in hopping into it. Nipper scooped him up and zipped him in, then hung the tote over his other shoulder.

He scaled the ladder quickly. When he reached the top, he used one hand and pushed up on the round hatch above him. Sunlight flooded into the shaft. He climbed the last few rungs and peeked out of the opening.

He was back in the courtyard outside the Temple of Horus, atop the big stone statue of the bird-headed god.

"Falcon's nest," said Nipper.

He looked around the courtyard. To his left was a huge, M-shaped building covered with ancient carvings. To his right were the glass doors leading to the museum. Nipper slid down the bird statue's back and landed on his feet. Then he adjusted his backpack and his tote and walked into the museum.

"Greetings, young American boy," said a woman by the door.

"*Shukraan*," said Nipper.

The woman smiled at him.

"Very well spoken," she said.

Nipper smiled back. Just knowing how to say *please* and *thank you* in someone else's language really opened doors.

"What is in the tote bag?" she asked.

"It's a lamp," Nipper answered.

The woman studied the cone sticking out of the top of the bag. She watched Dennis's nose twitch several times.

"A dog . . . lamp," she said slowly. "I have a cat clock at home. Eyes move back and forth as the tail swings. Do you like cats?"

Dennis growled softly.

The woman looked concerned, and Nipper coughed several times to cover up the sound of the pug growling.

"Sorry," said Nipper. "I'm allergic to cats."

"Have a wonderful time in the museum, then," said the woman, waving him along.

Nipper walked around the corner quickly.

"Yankees lose again!"

The voice of a baseball announcer rang out. Nipper looked around, startled. Where was that coming from? He walked quickly past rows of statues and glass cases filled with pottery, tools, and other artifacts. He turned the corner and entered the same exhibit hall that he and Samantha had visited the last time they'd been in Egypt. A fancy tapestry hung on display here. Nipper remembered that it illustrated the story of "The Traveler and the Monkey King." Supposedly, a man was in trouble until a brave young girl rescued him with her red magic spear.

A man sat in a chair beside a table in one corner of the room. Nipper recognized him immediately. It was the museum guide who had translated the Monkey King story for him before. A small radio, about the size of a juice box, rested on the table. The man stared at the device, listening intently. Nipper could tell he wasn't paying attention to anything else in the room, including him or Dennis.

"*Final score: Red Sox, twenty-two. Yankees, zero!*"

"*Rahib,*" said the man. "That makes one hundred and forty-six losses in a row."

He switched off the radio, sighed heavily, and began massaging his forehead with one hand. He noticed Nipper and stopped.

"I know you," he said, pointing at Nipper. "You're that super-annoying boy who came in here a few months ago."

Nipper nodded.

"Where's your sister?" the guide asked.

"She wouldn't come with me," said Nipper. "She's too busy to help with my mission."

"Mission, eh?" replied the guide. "Good thing you brought that dog."

"You mean this lamp?" said Nipper.

"I can see it's a dog with a plastic cone," said the guide.

"Oh, *this* dog," said Nipper, setting the tote bag on the floor.

Dennis walked out of the bag and sat on the floor, looking up at the guide.

"When I'm in trouble, he always saves the day," said Nipper.

The man seemed to study the dog for a while.

"Do you think the dog saves you because you are friends?" he asked. "Or does he think you are going to drop snacks around him?"

"Probably both," said Nipper. "But right now I'm here to save my Yankees from grave danger."

"*Your* Yankees?" asked the guide.

"Yeah," said Nipper. "I was the owner of the team, until the girl in the house next to me stole them."

"Girl?" asked the guide. "Describe this girl. Is she young? Is she old?"

"Well . . . she's mean," said Nipper. "And she always wears the same yellow polka-dot blouse."

"A mean girl in a yellow polka-dot blouse. Young . . .

or maybe old," the guide repeated slowly, considering each word.

"Yeah," said Nipper. "And she's tricky, too. Every time I try to get back my team, I wind up losing more things and . . . Wait. Is that a Yankees pin?"

The guide glanced down at his shirt. A shiny letter N with a Y in the middle—the logo of the New York Yankees—sparkled on his pocket.

"It certainly is, young American boy," he told Nipper proudly. "I wear it every day, even when it's not baseball season. I am a big fan of the Bronx Bombers."

"You are?" asked Nipper.

"The biggest," said the guide. "Many of my friends have given up on them because of the losing streak, but not me. I am a true Yankees fan, and I listen to *every* game on my Internet radio."

He pointed at his chest with his thumb.

"I wear this pin to show everyone I still believe in the team," he said. "The Yankees are the best."

"I believe, too," said Nipper. "I really do."

They both looked at each other for a long silent moment.

"The Yankees are the best! The best! The best!" they chanted together.

"So turn the radio back on," said Nipper. "Game one hundred forty-seven is starting soon."

The museum guide flipped the switch.

"It's a triple! The Boston Red Sox come out swinging!"

"Rahib!" the man shouted, and he switched the radio off again.

Nipper looked confused.

"That means 'terrible' in Arabic," the guide explained. "I am so very worried that this game will be their last. You know about rule thirteen hundred thirteen, section thirteen, don't you?"

"I sure do," said Nipper. "That's why I'm here. I'm going to end their losing streak once and for all."

"You?" asked the guide. "How will you accomplish this?"

Nipper pulled the ring from his pocket.

"An arachnid," the man observed. "Do you think this ring is the reason for the Yankees' losing streak?"

"Yes. It came from a secret place under this museum," Nipper explained. "And it spread a terrible curse on my Yankees."

The guide's eyes widened.

"I'm going back down there," said Nipper.

"I've always thought there were more secrets to this museum," the man said. "I've been planning to take a closer look at things."

"I'm going to drop the ring," said Nipper. "Into a bottomless pit."

"Bottomless?" asked the man.

"Yeah," Nipper answered. "The pit doesn't go anywhere. The ring will fall forever."

"Everything is connected to something. . . . Or so I've heard," said the guard.

"Come along with me," said Nipper. "We can save the team together."

"I wish I could," said the guide. "But I am on duty."

Nipper smiled. He always thought it was funny when police or firefighters or security guards said they were—

"Yes, young man," said the museum guide. "I said *on duty*. I know you're just trying to inject a little humor, but I take my job seriously."

He flipped the switch on the radio again.

"Base hit! The Red Sox lead, two to zero!"

"Rahib!" shouted Nipper. "I've got to go right now."

He turned and started to leave.

"Waitaminute," said the guide.

He held out the small radio.

"Take this with you," he told Nipper. "You can follow the team while you save them."

"Thanks so much," said Nipper.

"Just don't keep the radio on the whole time," said the guide. "The battery isn't very good. You'll run out of power. Understand?"

Nipper nodded. He reached back and unzipped the top of his backpack. He slid the radio inside the pack.

Then he fished around and pulled out the old baseball glove that Uncle Paul had given him.

"I want you to have this," he said to the guard. "A special present for a fellow true Yankees fan."

"Are you sure you won't need to catch anything on your mission down below?" asked the guide.

Nipper shrugged. "Nah," he said. "I don't think I'll need it. The only thing I'm really worried about is not making it there in time to save my team."

"Good luck," said the guide, taking the glove from him.

He slipped it onto his right hand and waved.

"I will be rooting for you as much as I root for the Yankees," he added.

"*Shukraan,*" said Nipper.

He left the gallery and headed to the section of the museum with two rows of columns. There he found the ceremonial riverboat he'd discovered on his last trip. He walked around the rectangular pedestal, pressing on each side as he went. On the third try, the panel clicked and swung inward.

"Let's go," he said to Dennis.

Then he crouched and crawled inside the opening.

CHAPTER THIRTY-NINE

A TOMB WITH A VIEW

Nipper inched forward through the dimly lit hall. The only light came from the gaps around the panel behind him, so the farther he crawled, the darker it became. Soon he was in total darkness.

He stopped crawling and reached over his shoulder. He unzipped his backpack and fumbled around inside until he felt the headlamp he had borrowed from his dad's office, and he pulled it out. He twisted a knob on the side of the square bulb, and it lit up.

"Wruf!" barked Dennis, and the incredibly bright bulb in his dog collar switched on.

"Gaah!" Nipper exclaimed, dropping the headlamp and covering his face with his hands. "Off, off!"

"Wruf!" the dog barked again, and the light switched off.

Nipper uncovered his eyes. He picked up the headlamp and stretched the elastic band around his head, illuminating the hallway. It was about three feet high and the walls were smooth. The bright lights revealed that he'd already crawled about a third of the way to their destination.

Nipper reached into the backpack again, took out the radio, and flipped the switch.

"And that's the end of the third inning. The Yankees trail the Red Sox by three!"

"Okay, follow me," he said to Dennis. "Let's go."

He switched off the radio and started crawling down the tunnel again. There were only six innings to go.

Slowly he made his way through the tunnel, dust sparkling in the beam of the headlamp. Then, a *flash!* A shaft of bright light beamed into the tunnel, and Nipper froze. He relaxed when he remembered that mirrors lined the chamber ahead. He climbed to his feet. Then, cautiously, he stepped through the opening into an eerie round room.

Beams of light bounced in every direction. Every surface glowed.

Except for the floor.

In the center of the room was a horrible black circular void.

But that was okay, he reminded himself. It was the reason why he had traveled so far to reach this place.

"It's almost goodbye time," Nipper said, patting his front pocket as if the emerald scorpion could hear him.

The room was just as it had been the last time he'd been there. The floor surrounding the pit was lined with cracked clay tiles and a layer of dried crud. Nipper scanned the walls, which were covered in carvings of fish, birds, sea creatures, and skulls. He thought the Egyptian art in the temple and museum above was interesting and cool. Down here, everything was strange and creepy.

Between the carvings, silver mirrors hung from brackets on the walls, reflecting rays of light around the chamber. Nipper guessed that this is what it would feel like to be inside a disco ball. It made him uncomfortable. He really didn't like being inside balls anymore.

He flipped the switch on the radio.

"*Triple play! The Yankees are out at first, second, and third base!*"

Nipper's heart raced. Was that the end of the game?

"*As we go to the top of the fifth, the score is Boston, three, New York . . . zero.*"

He let out a sigh of relief and switched off the radio. "I made it with five innings to spare."

Nipper inched forward to the edge of the pit. He pictured himself covered with goo, slipping and sliding toward this pit the last time he was there. If Samantha hadn't pinned his shirt to the floor with her umbrella, he would have tumbled over the edge. *He* would have disappeared forever.

Dennis growled softly, watching him approach the pit.

"It's okay," said Nipper. "I'm not going into that hole."

Dennis kept growling.

Nipper reached into his backpack and felt the box of granola bars. He took out two and tossed them onto the floor in front of Dennis.

"You stay here," said Nipper. "Have a snack . . . and keep quiet."

Nipper turned back to face the pit. Carefully he leaned over and peered into the darkness. He could see maybe twenty feet down. Was it as bottomless as he thought? He reached into his pocket and took out the shiny, silver-colored penny Uncle Paul had given him. He held it out over the pit, let go, and waited.

And waited.

And waited.

There was no sound. But did that mean the pit was truly bottomless, or was it just so deep that anything you dropped was way out of hearing range before it touched the bottom? Nipper figured it didn't really matter. He was pretty sure that once something went in there, it was gone for good. That was his plan.

It was time.

Nipper reached into his pocket again and felt the sharp point of the emerald scorpion's pincers. He pulled the evil ring from his pocket and examined it.

The cursed thing had come from this place. Now he was going to make sure it stayed down here for good.

Dennis had begun growling again, but Nipper ignored him.

"Here goes everything," he said.

Nipper closed his eyes and stretched his arm out over the big dark pit.

"So long, evil ancient Egyptian curse," he said. "One . . . two . . . two and a half . . ."

And something snatched the ring from his hand.

CHAPTER FORTY

MINE

Boy has a shiny bug ring.

I take it.

"Breep!"

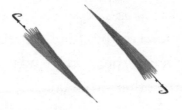

CHAPTER FORTY-ONE

FINDERS BREEPERS

Nipper opened his eyes just in time to see a hairy hand sweep past his face.

It was the monkey!

It was the monkey from the RAIN. The monkey who had also starred in Buffy's musical play, and who had attacked Nipper with a peanut gun at the elephant-shaped building in New Jersey and chased him into the *kogelbaan*.

And it had just stolen the ring!

"*Breep!*"

Nipper stood, stunned, and watched the animal scamper around to the opposite side of the pit. There it stopped and began dancing as it waved the ring in the air.

"Bring . . . that . . . back!" shouted Nipper.

He sprinted around the pit, but when he reached the other side of the room, the monkey was where Nipper had started. On the other side again.

"Bring . . . *yourself* . . . back!" shouted Nipper.

He dashed around the pit again—he was determined to get that monkey—but the monkey bounded away from the pit and toward a second doorway. Nipper ran as fast as he could, but the backpack slowed him down. And the monkey was fast!

"No! No! No!" Nipper wailed as the monkey zipped around the corner into another room.

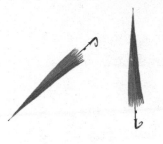

CHAPTER FORTY-TWO

PUG PATROL

Dennis sat in the doorway.
"Wruf! Wruf!"
The bright light went on and off.
Dennis barked at the boy and the monkey.
He wanted to help the boy. . . .
But the boy had told him to stay.
He wanted to help the boy. . . .
But the boy had put granola bars on the floor.
Dennis stayed and ate the granola bars.

The granola bars were sweet.
The granola bars were gone.
The boy was gone.

Dennis waited for a while.
The boy didn't come back.

Dennis went into another room.
Shiny things were everywhere.
Dennis licked a shiny thing.
It was salty.
Dennis licked another shiny thing.
It was salty, too.
Dennis licked.
Dennis licked and licked.

CHAPTER FORTY-THREE

WHO'S THERE?

Nipper dashed after the monkey into a new room—and stopped. The monkey was gone.

Nipper bent forward, resting his hands on his knees, and tried to catch his breath.

"How . . . incredibly . . . awful," he panted.

But this was more than awful. It was a catastrophe. He'd been so close to saving his Yankees. And now this! He stood up straight and caught his breath.

He remembered this room well. It was the place where he and Samantha had thought Uncle Paul had exploded. Here they had opened the secret panel and discovered a letter written for his sister.

"I didn't miss opening day," Nipper said, remembering

the instructions from his uncle when he'd gotten the team as a present.

But now Nipper was missing *closing day*. This was going to be the last time his Yankees took to the field. Nobody would wear the awesome pin-striped uniforms again. Nobody except for . . .

"Musical theater!" he said loudly, and as his words echoed back to him, he began to survey all the walls of the room.

Nearly every surface was covered in hanging fabric.

He took a closer look.

Below one tapestry, close to the wall, two circus peanuts lay on the floor.

Nipper smiled.

He walked over and tugged on the tapestry. It snapped free from the ceiling and fell to the floor, revealing a wall covered in a grid of square white stones. Each square looked to be about two feet across, and featured a different strange carving: sea creatures, anchors, parrots, skulls, swords, and boats. None of them seemed very Egyptian at all.

Nipper ran his fingers across the panels as he explored. Samantha always complained that he poked and touched everything, and that it was super-annoying, but this was serious business.

When he touched the panel featuring a sailing ship,

he stopped. It *looked* like it was made of white stone, but it *felt* different. This square was made of wood.

He pressed his ear to the panel.

Nothing.

He stepped back from the wall and stared at the square. It was definitely a different color from all the others. He reached out and banged on the panel.

Knock-knock!

He waited.

"Breep, breep?" a muffled voice squeaked from behind the panel.

Nipper thought about it for a second.

"Hugh," he answered.

"Breep breep?" the voice squeaked from behind the panel again.

Nipper pushed one side of the panel, and the other side swung outward.

"Hugh better give me back that ring!" Nipper shouted.

Swish!

A ninja throwing star flew from the opening in the wall, and sailed directly past Nipper's head, so close that he felt the rush of air against his cheek.

"Yaaaah!" Nipper screamed as he dove headfirst through the open panel.

Wham!

He tackled the monkey and grabbed on to it with both arms. The impact knocked off his dad's head-lamp, and they tumbled over each other, a ball of ninja monkey and true Yankees fan, and rolled into the darkness.

CHAPTER FORTY-FOUR

AMAZON PRIMATE

Nipper felt the monkey slipping through his grip. Then *wham!*

Nipper landed on his back . . . hard! His backpack cushioned some of the blow, but it still hurt a lot. And it *really* hurt where the Mickey Mantle bobblehead jabbed into his shoulder.

He heard footsteps and sat up quickly. The monkey was scampering away.

"Hello?" he called.

Silence.

It was too dark to see much of anything. He felt around with both hands.

Wet sand.

He stood up.

"Hello?" Nipper called again.

Nothing.

This was a strange new room. It had a muddy floor of some kind.

He listened carefully and heard the sound of rushing water.

Nipper stepped forward and stopped. His foot sank into shallow water.

He looked around again.

A few feet away, a glowing rectangle caught his eye.

"Headlamp . . . check," said Nipper with a sigh of relief.

His dad's headlamp rested, lens-down, in the sand. Nipper walked over, picked it up, and put it back on his head.

With the bright lamp lighting the space around him, he could see that he wasn't in just another room at all. He had tumbled into some vast underground cavern. Nipper was standing on the bank of a wide underground river.

And, in the distance, the monkey was paddling away in a canoe!

Quickly Nipper took in his surroundings. A second canoe lay beached on the shore. Wasting no time, he dragged the boat into the water, picked up an oar, and began paddling as hard as he could after the monkey thief.

The current was stronger than Nipper had expected. It took a lot of strength to keep from being swept sideways and carried away from the monkey. But his Yankees needed him, so he stayed focused.

Water swirled and splattered as Nipper paddled furiously.

"Come back!" he shouted at the monkey in the distance.

He wanted to turn the radio on to check the game, but he didn't dare stop paddling. The monkey was almost to the other side, and Nipper couldn't let it get away. Sweat rolled down his forehead as he moved furiously, fighting the strong current.

Ahead he could see that the monkey had reached the shore of the river and was now climbing onto something shaped like a long rectangle. Just as it started to inch forward, Nipper realized what it was. The monkey had boarded a double mine cart. It looked a lot like the one that he and Sam had ridden in the salt mine under Detroit. The monkey was rolling away!

A bright green dot blinked in the distance. The ring was rolling away, too!

"Come back!" Nipper shouted again as he hopped out of the canoe and splashed ashore.

Once again, the monkey didn't answer him. It didn't really matter, though. Nipper was pretty sure that if it had, the reply would have been: *"Breep!"*

CHAPTER FORTY-FIVE

END OF THE LINE

Nipper scrambled up the muddy shore and reached the tracks.

The double cart with the monkey was almost out of sight, but he could still see the blinking green dot of the evil scorpion ring.

He spotted a side branch of the rail system with a single mine cart parked on it.

He raced up to it and peeked inside. The cart was similar to the one he and his sister had ridden in the salt mine. But this one didn't have a motor.

"Never mine," said Nipper.

He started to chuckle to himself about his joke, then stopped. Would Samantha have thought it was funny? She probably wouldn't have. She'd probably say it was "kid-brother funny," which really meant, "I can't tell if it's funny or not because I'm too busy trying to save my uncle to laugh at anything." Nipper planned to test it out on her after he saved his Yankees.

He grabbed on to one side of the cart and began pushing it forward. It rolled onto the main track and started to accelerate. Nipper pulled himself up the side of the rolling cart, but as he climbed over the edge, his muddy wet shoes slipped.

Whomp!

He flopped into the cart.

As he lay on his back, his headlamp illuminated the ceiling of the cavern, or tunnel, or whatever he was rolling through. He watched it pass faster and faster as the cart accelerated. Everything rattled around him. It made his teeth hurt. He pulled himself up and faced forward.

His headlamp illuminated the track and—

Nipper gasped. About thirty feet ahead, the rails stopped, jutting out into the air. The track was about to end!

"I'm on a train to—"

There was no time to jump out . . . but there was plenty of time to scream.

"No-o-o-o-o-o . . . ," Nipper shouted as the cart zipped off the end of the track, ". . . whe-e-e-re!"

Gripping the sides of the rolling metal bin, he dropped like a big screaming bag of salt.

CHAPTER FORTY-SIX

TRACK TO THE FUTURE

Clank!

The cart slammed down onto a new set of tracks. Nipper fell forward and crashed onto the cart's metal flooring. Slowly he stood back up and steadied himself by holding on to the sides of the cart.

Sparks flew as it skidded down a new, even steeper incline. Wind whipped at his hair as he zoomed along. Glancing over the side of the cart, he saw that the tracks ran along the riverbank. The water churned and roiled.

He looked ahead again. In the distance, the double mine cart rolled in front of him—about thirty feet ahead on the track! The monkey was in the front cart, jumping up and down, waving the green emerald ring. Nipper thought he saw it flash between two hairy fingers.

Jeremy Bernard Spinner, also known as Nipper, knew more than anyone else on planet Earth about accidently dropping valuable items. From old comic books to fancy pocket watches to big blue diamonds, he had lost them all. And now, as the monkey jumped and flailed in the cart ahead, Nipper knew one thing for certain: that animal was going to drop that ring any second!

He had to catch up with the monkey. But how?

The wind whipped at his hair as he raced along. Nipper thought about all the magtrain and pneumatic tube travel he'd done recently. If he had learned anything, it was . . .

"Watch out for the WIND!" shouted Nipper.

He ducked low so he could just barely peek over the front of the cart. With less air resistance, he sped up and began gaining on the monkey.

Thirty feet . . .

The monkey was still facing forward. He didn't seem to notice Nipper approaching—or maybe he didn't care. He waved the ring, hopping up and down in his cart.

Nipper stared at the scorpion ring with a feeling of dread. That animal was *really* being careless!

Beyond the monkey, something caught Nipper's eye. In the distance, the track divided into two, and the paths curved away from each other, leading into two different tunnels. And standing on the side of the tracks up ahead was a big metal arrow on a pole pointed to the left. Lower on the pole, a bright orange handle stuck out, ready to switch the direction of the track.

Nipper looked ahead to the tunnel on the right. Over the entrance was a sign:

WATCH OUT FOR THE WIND!

"I know that already," said Nipper.

Another banner came into view. It was a white skull with bones sticking out of it in eight directions, on a black background.

Nipper recognized it immediately. It was the same banner he'd seen in Missy's creepy basement, flying from the mast of the pirate ship in the painting.

Was it something important? Did that symbol have something to do with the WIND? Samantha was going to really want to know about this! He stuck out his hand, ready to grab the handle and make the track point to the right.

"Breep!"

He looked to his left. The double cart with the monkey had already rolled past the junction. Nipper watched the monkey disappearing into the left-hand tunnel. The green ring flashed in the darkness.

Then he looked back at the sign.

Twenty feet . . .

Nipper flipped the switch on the radio.

"Home run! It's the top of seventh inning, and the Red Sox continue to lead, four to zero!"

Nipper let out a heavy sigh, switched off the radio, and shoved it into a side pocket of his backpack. He couldn't go both ways, and his Yankees needed him.

He watched the lever go past.

"Sorry, Sam," said Nipper as the cart zoomed past the junction into the left-hand tunnel.

He glanced at the mysterious skull and the warning about the WIND. He watched them disappear behind him as he rolled farther into the dark tunnel.

Then he faced forward again.

Ten feet . . .

"Breep!" the monkey howled.

Nipper climbed up onto the front of his rolling metal vehicle. The extra weight on the front caused sparks to spray up from the wheels like fireworks.

He took a deep breath. . . .

And jumped.

CHAPTER FORTY-SEVEN

GRAND SLAM

Thump!

Nipper landed on his feet in the back half of the monkey's double cart.

"Give me that ring!" he shouted over the roaring wind.

The monkey stared back at Nipper, then looked down at the connector between the two mine carts. It reached forward and yanked out the metal pin that had held the two together, and the vehicles began to separate.

"Oh, no you don't!" Nipper shouted, and sprang forward again.

This time he didn't slip. He grabbed the back of the cart and swung his legs up and over the edge, and landed right in front of the monkey.

Without the weight of the second cart, the front cart with the boy and the monkey began to speed up.

Nipper stepped forward and . . .

SCRA-A-A-A-A-PE!

The cart tilted forward with Nipper's weight, and its rear wheels left the track, sending him sliding into the hairy beast.

"Breep!" the creature screamed, less than an inch from Nipper's face.

Nipper smelled candy peanuts on the monkey's breath, along with smoldering paint and metal from the sparks that were flying everywhere. He closed his eyes and imagined the smell of popcorn and soft pretzels on a sunny day in Yankee Stadium. A crowd was cheering and the organ played as . . .

Nipper opened his eyes.

No. If he didn't save his Yankees now, that could never, ever happen again!

He reached out, placed an arm on either side of the monkey, and pushed against the front of the cart, shoving himself backward.

Clang!

The mine cart's rear wheels slammed back onto the track.

"It's a high fly ball . . . and it's caught!"

The jolt had bumped the switch on the radio. It blared from the side pocket of Nipper's backpack.

"Seventh-inning stretch! Let's all sing a rousing chorus of 'Take Me Out to the—' "

Ka-clunk!

The mine cart rolled over a bump in the track, and the radio turned off.

Nipper didn't know if he should panic because his Yankees only had two and a half innings left, or if he should cheer because he didn't have to sing "Take Me Out to the Ball Game." He really hated that song!

His knees shook. Nine more outs until his Yankees were done. He stared into the monkey's reddish-brown eyes and then at the bright green ring in its hand. Somehow the creature still held it between its hairy thumb and index finger.

The monkey growled.

No. It wasn't the monkey. It was Nipper's stomach. He began to think about the granola bars in his backpack.

"Maximum time limit exceeded!" he shouted.

The monkey stared, looking puzzled.

Nipper reached over his shoulder and tugged the backpack zipper open with one hand. He fished around inside, grabbed a granola bar, and held it out in front of him.

"Take this," he said.

When the monkey reached for the treat, Nipper pulled his hand back.

"Ring," he demanded.

"Breep," said the monkey.

Nipper pointed to the emerald scorpion in the monkey's other hand.

"Ring," he repeated.

"Breep," repeated the monkey, dangling the ring.

Slowly Nipper held out the granola bar.

The monkey licked its lips . . . and snatched it!

Nipper watched silently as the monkey shoved the whole granola bar into its mouth, chewed furiously, and swallowed.

"Ring," Nipper said once again.

The monkey picked a few granola crumbs from the corners of its mouth and stared.

"May I have the ring now?" asked Nipper.

The monkey stared at him.

"Please," Nipper added.

The monkey swung his head from side to side.

Nipper's stomach growled.

No . . . , it wasn't his stomach. It was Nipper, growling with rage!

"A granola bar wasn't enough for you?" he shouted.

He reached behind his back.

"Well, that's okay! I have a whole *pack*!" he shouted.

"Bree—"

Wham!

Nipper whirled around, swinging the backpack with one hand and slamming it into the monkey.

A cloud of board game parts, tokens, and dice erupted from the pack. Colorful play money swirled and fluttered. Arms, legs, and the head from the Mickey Mantle bobblehead flew out, too.

The monkey tumbled out of the cart . . . and the ring sailed up into the air!

Nipper shot out his free hand.

He grabbed the ring and held tight!

"Gotcha," said Nipper.

He looked down and saw the monkey plunge into the raging river below. Quickly, Nipper shoved the ring into his pocket and put the pack on his back again.

Clack!

The cart rolled over some kind of switch, and suddenly lurched onto a different track. Nipper craned his neck, trying to look back to the river, but he couldn't see it anymore.

Clack!

The cart rolled over another switch and swerved onto another track.

Nipper was still trying to find the river. He wanted to know what had happened to the monkey. He faced forward again to see—that he was heading straight into a wall!

There was no time to jump out of the cart!

CRASH!

The mine cart smashed through the wall. Bricks,

tiles, rocks, and splintered wooden beams flew everywhere. Dirt, dust, and ancient paint flakes filled the air.

The cart zipped along, and the dusty cloud began to clear.

Nipper realized he was back in the round chamber . . . and he was rolling straight toward the bottomless pit!

He threw his body against the rear of the cart. It flipped back.

CLANG!

SCRA-A-A-A-A-PE!

The cart skidded to a stop, inches from the edge of the pit.

"Wruf!" barked Dennis, trotting up to the cart.

The Blinky Barker light switched on, blasting Nipper with light.

"Off!" ordered Nipper.

"Wruf!" barked Dennis.

Nipper took off the backpack and tossed it out of the cart.

"It's the bottom of the eighth inning with two outs!"

The radio had switched on again.

"The Red Sox still lead, four to zero!"

He rolled out of the upended cart and onto the chamber floor, stood up, and took a deep breath.

"Stay," he told Dennis.

Calmly Nipper walked to the pit's edge. He took the scorpion ring from his pocket, raised it over his head, and threw the ring, straight down, as hard as he could.

The emerald scorpion flashed once before it disappeared into darkness.

CHAPTER FORTY-EIGHT

BOTTOMLESS PITCH

Nipper stared into the pit and waited.

He saw nothing. He heard nothing.

"It's a base hit for the Yankees!"

He looked up. The radio blared from inside his backpack. He held his breath and waited.

"Home run!"

The announcer began to call hit after hit after hit. Nipper ran over to the pack.

"Home run! . . . Triple! . . . Home run!"

He sat down beside his backpack and listened to the radio.

"Single! . . . Single! . . . Single! . . . Grand slam!"

His Yankees were scoring so many runs, Nipper lost

track of the score. It was magical! He felt like his head might explode . . . with joy!

"It's a home run! . . . And another home run! . . . Home run! . . . Home—"

The radio cut off. Its batteries were dead.

Nipper's batteries were dead, too. He was exhausted . . . but it was over!

It was over. His plan had worked. The Yankees were going to win, and they weren't going to get kicked out of the league, and their bats weren't going to get chopped into firewood. And no musical theater!

He stood up, brushed sand from his pants, and grabbed his backpack. He had to get back up to the museum. As tired as he was, Nipper wanted to celebrate with a fellow true Yankees fan.

CHAPTER FORTY-NINE

RAHIB!

Nipper marched triumphantly into the exhibit hall.

The guide stood by his table with an eager expression on his face.

"Well?" he asked.

"Yankees win," said Nipper. "I did it. *We* did it."

"Wonderful, wonderful news," said the man.

Nipper held out the radio.

"The battery died," he said.

"Give it to me," the man answered quickly. "I'll plug it in."

Nipper put the radio on the table, and the guide reached for a power cable dangling from a nearby outlet.

"Turn it on, turn it on," Nipper chanted eagerly.

"I can't wait to hear the postgame celebration," said the guide as he switched on the radio.

"*What an amazing game, folks! The Yankees scored a dozen runs.*"

"And?" said Nipper to the radio.

"And?" the guide repeated.

"*And then the Boston Red Sox came roaring back! They scored two hundred runs in the ninth inning. What a victory for Boston!*"

Nipper and the guide looked at each other, stunned.

"*And with their one hundred and forty-seventh loss, the New York Yankees will have to leave Major League Baseball. Their bats will become firewood, and their uniforms will become costumes for musical—*"

Nipper reached out and grabbed the radio. He tugged, pulling it free from the power cord.

He and the guide stared at each other in shock. Their heads looked like they were going to explode. For almost a minute, the two true Yankees fans stood together in silence.

"Hey," said Nipper, glancing around the room. "Where's that old baseball glove I gave you?"

"Ugh," said the guide. "I lost it. I'm so embarrassed. I hope it wasn't very valuable."

"Don't worry about it," said Nipper. "If nobody ever lost anything, nothing would be valuable. At least, that's what my uncle Paul always says."

The guide nodded. He reached for the Yankees pin on his shirt.

For a moment, Nipper thought the man was going to remove the pin. Instead he polished it with his thumb.

"I think someone needs you," he said.

"My sister?" asked Nipper. "Nah. She'll do just fine without me. My dad'll help her with math or light-bulbs."

"No," said the guide. "Your lamp-dog. I think you left him somewhere."

"Whoops," said Nipper, turning. "I'll be right back."

"See you again soon, young fellow Yankee fan," the guard called as Nipper rushed out of the room.

CHAPTER FIFTY

SHATTERED

"Dennis!" Nipper called as he entered the pit room. "Time to go home!"

His voice echoed as he searched the room for the pug. No one was there.

"Dennis?" Nipper repeated. "I said it's time to . . ."

He looked at the pit and gulped. Had the pug fallen in?

Nipper stepped to the edge of the hole. He squinted into the darkness. It sure looked bottomless . . . and useless. In spite of everything, his Yankees were done.

But it would be truly horrible if—in addition to not saving his team and not helping his sister—he'd gone and lost their dog.

"Dennis?" he called again.

As he stared into the darkness, he heard a faint scratching, tapping sound.

Nipper looked over his shoulder. The sound was coming from around the corner, the exit across from where he had followed the monkey. He left the pit's edge and walked through the doorway quickly.

Nipper entered a room that he remembered very well. It was a treasure room filled with statues, trophies, jewels, and furniture. Shiny metal masks were stacked in a neat pile. A woven basket had tipped over, scattering dozens of huge red gems and gold coins across the tile floor. Everything glinted in the light of Nipper's headlamp.

When they'd first discovered this underground tomb, Nipper had wanted to bring a bunch of loot home so he could buy his team back. Samantha had convinced him it was a bad idea to take anything out of this place. She couldn't have been more right about it. All he'd taken was one lousy ring, and it had wrecked his life!

At the far end of the room, Dennis's cone tapped against the lower part of a tall flat panel as he scratched at it with his front paws. The surfboard-shaped stone was the lid to a mummy case propped up against the wall. The pug alternated between scratching at the lid and licking flecks of powder that he had scraped free with his paws. Nipper could tell the dog had been at it for quite a while. The bottom of the lid looked like Dennis had worn some of it away with his sharp toenails.

"What are you doing, pal?" asked Nipper, stepping forward.

Crunch!

Nipper looked down. He'd stepped on a ruby, and it had crushed under his foot.

"Fake?" asked Nipper.

He knelt down and studied the crushed stone. All that was left of it was a clump of pink powder.

Nipper stood back up and looked around the room. How much of the treasure in this room was real?

He stepped to the side and bumped into a low table, toppling a statue of a bird.

Crash!

The statue hit the floor and shattered into a hundred dusty fragments. Nipper scratched his head. It was a fake, too. What else in this room wasn't a real treasure?

Next to him, on the ground, was a bundle of long slender rods. They were carved with elaborate geometric shapes. They looked like magic wands, the kind wizards used in storybooks.

Nipper brought his foot down on the sticks, and *crunch,* they crumbled into small chips of sparkling white powder. He knelt down and touched the powder with his finger. He brought it to his tongue. It tasted salty. He crushed the rest of the wands into powder. It was *all* made of salt!

Cree-e-eak. Smash!

The heavy sarcophagus lid fell sideways and crashed onto the floor of the chamber, exploding into pieces and sending up a cloud of white salt flakes. They swirled around the room like a dusty snow flurry.

"Watch out for the SNOW," Nipper said quietly.

The SNOW had been here. Somehow they had found a way to get in and out of this place, and they were using the room to store all their phony, salty treasure.

Nipper looked back to the doorway that led to the pit room, and his eyes went wide.

"Everything is connected to something," said Nipper.

He looked across the chamber at Dennis. The pug licked furiously at a chunk of the shattered sarcophagus lid.

"Come on, pal," said Nipper.

"Wruf?" the dog barked, switching on the Blinky Barker light.

"Off, off," said Nipper, shielding his eyes from the bulb's intense glare.

"Wruf," Dennis barked again. The light turned off, and the little dog followed him through the door back to the big round room.

"It's too late to save my Yankees," said Nipper, walking to the edge of the pit. "But maybe it's not too late to save my sister."

He stepped forward, picked up Dennis, and then walked to the mine cart that still sat next to the pit. The pug began to squirm.

"Relax, pal," said Nipper, climbing into the cart with the dog. "I have an idea."

He peered over the front of the cart, and into the blackness of the pit. Then he began to shift his weight, causing the cart to rock back to front.

"Wruf!" Dennis barked nervously.

The cart began inching forward.

Dennis kept struggling, but Nipper held him tightly to his chest.

"Here goes . . . everything!" Nipper shouted.

The cart rolled over the edge and dropped into the pit.

CHAPTER FIFTY-ONE

INTERMURAL

"Remember," Samantha said as she and her father headed up the steps inside the main hall of the Detroit Institute of Arts. "Everything we're doing is still super-secret. Try not to draw attention to us."

She glanced over at the tall black top hat bobbing on her father's head, then looked down at the red umbrella she carried with her on a sunny summer day.

Oh well. They would do their best not to stick out too much.

"I'll be careful," said Mr. Spinner, adjusting his hat. "I'm just here to help with any math challenges we may encounter."

They reached the entrance to the courtyard of the *Detroit Industry Murals*.

"And of course I'm prepared to handle any lightbulb challenges that may confront us on our journey," he added.

They hadn't discussed lightbulbs on the trip from Seattle to Detroit. There hadn't been any "lightbulb challenges" on the *kogelbaan* or during the salt mine ride. Samantha couldn't imagine any during this particular trip. But her father was senior lightbulb tester at the American Institute of Lamps, so she knew he'd bring it up sooner or later.

It sure wasn't one-hundredth of a percent as annoying as hearing Nipper talk about the Yankees.

"I wonder what the wattage is in these cases," Samantha's father said as they passed the suits of armor on display. "The color balance of the light is superb."

Okay. Maybe it was *one-quarter of a percent* as annoying as Nipper talking about the Yankees.

Again Samantha had the feeling that her dad cared about lightbulbs, her mom, math, Nipper, math, Buffy, breakfast making, and her, in that order. But that was okay for the moment. She needed him to help with math so that she could find Uncle Paul.

The room with the *Detroit Industry Murals* was more crowded than the last time Samantha had been there. Of course, today there was no phony blizzard warning from the SNOW.

"It's over there," said Samantha, pointing to the planter beneath the large mural with the machinery.

She led her father to the plastic plant and pointed to the red faucet handle.

"Most people are looking at the murals, so they don't notice anything strange about the water faucet," she told him.

Mr. Spinner touched one of the broad, flat leaves, and seemed to ponder something.

"Plastic plants," he said. "So there's no reason to have a faucet here."

"Exactly," said Samantha. "But don't touch it until we get everyone looking in another direction."

"How are we going to do that?" asked her father.

Samantha smiled. She stood up straight and pointed to the room's entrance.

"Wow! Look over there!" she shouted. "It's a famous billionaire internet movie star supermodel sports celebrity!"

Everyone in the courtyard turned to look at the entrance.

Samantha winked at her dad. Then she reached through the plant leaves, grabbed the faucet handle, and gave it a twist.

Chunka-chunka-chunka!

Samantha looked up at the mural. Once again the mighty machine had begun to move. It emerged from its camouflaged hiding place in the mural and lowered two mighty robot arms.

Clamp!

Clamp!

The arms grabbed Samantha and her father.

"Holy high candle power!" shouted Mr. Spinner.

Chunka!

And the machine yanked both of them into the wall.

CHAPTER FIFTY-TWO

SNOWBUDDY'S HOME

Chunka!

The mighty robot arm gently lowered Samantha onto the floor of a wide tunnel. She checked quickly to make sure she still had her umbrella over her shoulder.

Chunka!

Her father dropped beside her.

"That was like a roller coaster," said Mr. Spinner. "It's too bad Nipper wasn't here to enjoy it."

"He *was* here, Dad," said Samantha. "I was here, too."

"I remember how much that boy enjoyed our trip to Pacific Pandemonium, when he—"

"Look! There's math," Samantha interrupted, pointing behind him.

Once again she felt like her dad liked Nipper and lightbulbs more than he cared about her.

"Interesting," said her father, turning to face the wall.

He studied the grid of numbers for a few seconds. Then he began pressing panels.

"Come join me," he said. "I'll start at the top left."

Samantha used her umbrella to tap the number thirteen.

Together they pressed until twelve squares were lit with the Fibonacci sequence.

1	1	2	3	4	5	6	7	8	9	10	11	12	13	14	15	16
17	18	19	20	21	22	23	24	25	26	27	28	29	30	31	32	33
34	35	36	37	38	39	40	41	42	43	44	45	46	47	48	49	50
51	52	53	54	55	56	57	58	59	60	61	62	63	64	65	66	67
68	69	70	71	72	73	74	75	76	77	78	79	80	81	82	83	84
85	86	87	88	89	90	91	92	93	94	95	96	97	98	99	100	101
102	103	104	105	106	107	108	109	110	111	112	113	114	115	116	117	118
119	120	121	122	123	124	125	126	127	128	129	130	131	132	133	134	135
136	137	138	139	140	141	142	143	144	145	146	147	148	149	150	151	152

The lights on the wall began to blink.

"There was a clue here," said her father, stepping back from the wall. "The number one appears twice at the beginning. If you had known about the Fibonacci sequence, then you might have been able to guess."

The lights starting blinking faster and faster. . . .

Hiss-sssss!

The entire wall began to rise, like a giant garage door. Warm, salty air rushed out, and a tunnel was revealed, stretching out before Samantha and her father.

She estimated the tunnel to be twenty feet from side to side, and just as far from floor to ceiling. The smooth walls seemed to be carved from solid rock. Overhead, clusters of glowing crystals dangled, bathing the tunnel with soft light.

Statues lined the tunnel. Samantha recognized many of them from the ride through the salt mine. Others she recognized from all of Uncle Paul's stories.

"Michelangelo's *David*, Rodin's *The Thinker*," she said as they passed each iconic sculpture. "Abraham Lincoln, from the Lincoln Memorial." They were amazingly detailed replicas.

"Are these made of salt?" asked Samantha.

Her father stopped at a sculpture of a Chinese soldier. He rubbed it with his thumb.

"Not this one," he said. "It appears to be quartz."

He moved to a second soldier.

"This one might be marble," he said, squinting at the soldier's hat. "Amazing detail work."

Ahead of them, a lion sculpture seemed to stand guard on each side of the tunnel. Samantha recognized them. They were copies of the famous lions outside the New York Public Library in Manhattan.

Samantha shielded her eyes. In the distance, she could see that the tunnel opened into a much brighter chamber. She gestured for her father to join her behind the lion by the right wall of the tunnel. They both crouched and looked through the opening into the space beyond.

"Whoa, Nelly," Samantha whispered.

A vast, dome-shaped cavern stretched out ahead of them, shining as brightly as the world outside on a cloudless day. It reminded her of a basketball arena. Instead of a scoreboard, however, a cluster of hexagonal crystals dangled from the top of the dome. Each one looked to be about the size of the mailbox leading to the magtrain down the street from their house, and they glowed brightly.

"They must be using crystals to transfer light from the surface," said Mr. Spinner. "A high-tech alternate lighting system."

Samantha could tell that her father was both fascinated and delighted by the overhead lights, of course. But she was focused on the activity in the cavern. The chamber buzzed with motion. People in white coats and bright sneakers milled about.

"These are the strangers who took Uncle Paul, aren't they?" asked Samantha.

Her father nodded. Then he pointed to the rows of statues that continued all around the curved walls of the great dome. There were dozens of them, possibly more than a hundred.

"Let's do our best to keep out of sight," Samantha told her father.

They heard footsteps. A woman walked past the mouth of the tunnel and stopped. She stared at the open math wall. Samantha guessed she was trying to decide if it was supposed to be open or not.

Samantha and her father crouched lower behind the statue. The woman was close enough for them to read the writing on her coat:

$$yt + A(y)y_x = 0$$

"That's the formula for fluid under pressure," whispered Mr. Spinner.

"That's nice," Samantha whispered back. "But how are we going to go in there without being noticed?"

The SNOW woman shrugged, then scurried back to the center of the dome.

"Hold on," said Mr. Spinner.

He reached into his pocket and took out a small gadget. He flicked a button with his thumb, and it began to glow.

"*We're* under pressure, so we've got to be fluid," he said.

He pointed the self-powered light behind the lion

and studied the distance of the space between the statue and the wall of the tunnel.

"The gap is about two feet wide, enough for a person to pass through to the other side," he said.

He turned off the bulb, squeezed past the lion, and headed into the chamber.

"We can walk behind all these statues without getting stuck, and make our way around the dome without being seen," he said. "Follow me."

Okay, thought Samantha as she followed him. That *might* have just been a lightbulb challenge. She was glad she'd asked her father to come along . . . maybe.

The Detroit Salt Mines

In 1895, a huge deposit of rock salt was discovered beneath the city of Detroit, Michigan.

For over a century, workers have tunneled more than one thousand feet down and carved out a network of chambers covering more than five thousand acres. The vast excavation stretches all the way under the city, including downtown.

The mine is still active today, owned and operated by the Detroit Salt Company. Most of the salt harvested is sold as halite, rock salt used to de-ice streets during the winter.

* * *

The Detroit Salt Company is not the only organization tunneling under Detroit. A short distance from their salt mine, the Super-Numerical Overachievers Worldwide have carved out their own headquarters in the salty earth.

These math-minded criminals have created a huge subterranean dome where they can meet, exchange formulas, and practice making copies of valuable treasures.

The SNOW built their headquarters close to the salt mine so they can park their phony salt trucks without attracting attention. So far, no one has taken a closer look at the trucks. If they had, they would have found that the trucks around the museums have no salt inside them. They are filled instead with statues, artwork, and jewels—real ones coming out of the museums, and fake ones going in.

CHAPTER FIFTY-THREE

DOME SLEET DOME

Moving from statue to statue, the Spinners made their way around the dome.

They squeezed behind a replica of the Statue of Liberty, then behind one of the Greek goddess Selene. Samantha recognized about half the sculptures she saw. She had heard about them in school, seen pictures of them in books, or learned their stories from her uncle during one of his storytelling nights on the garage steps. Was Uncle Paul somewhere in this cavern?

Samantha and her father slid behind a statue of a man. The figure sat, bent over, measuring the ground with a compass.

"Isaac Newton," said Mr. Spinner. "A great mathematician, and an expert on light and lenses, too."

Samantha smiled. Of course her father knew that one.

Crouching, and peeking around the side of the statue, they began to get a more complete view of the SNOW headquarters. It was even bigger than Samantha had guessed, and it was much busier!

Men and women swarmed about the chamber. Some were carving and measuring new statues. They mostly worked using hammers and chisels, but a few SNOW agents chopped at the statues with strange tools. The devices looked like chainsaws but had blades of blazing blue-white light. Blue sparks flew around the agents as they worked, their green visors lowered to protect their eyes.

"What are those machines, Dad?" asked Samantha.

"I think . . . they're carving sculptures using some kind of high-energy plasma tools," he answered.

Samantha nodded. Did that count as another light-bulb challenge?

In the center of the dome, a dozen SNOW members stood before a billboard-sized whiteboard. They wrote and erased and chatted with each other. Samantha couldn't make out what they were writing, or hear what they were saying, but they seemed to be repeating long, complicated math formulas.

"*That* math class looks tough," said her father.

Farther across the dome, mine carts rolled in and out of the chamber. Samantha recognized the rolling metal bins from the ride through the salt mine. All along the tracks, SNOW members chopped at white boulders using picks and shovels. They filled bags with salt and tossed them onto passing trains.

Samantha tried to watch all the activity in the room,

but she found it hard to keep track. There was so much going on.

"Let's keep moving," she told her father.

They slipped behind a replica of the famous *Little Mermaid* from Denmark and continued their path around the SNOW dome.

After a dozen more statues, a shower of blue-white sparks stopped them in their tracks.

Samantha peeked out from behind a statue of a little girl who stood bravely with her hands on her hips. A few feet away, six SNOW men and women sat at workbenches, operating miniature versions of the high-energy plasma carvers the statue-makers used.

She squinted at one of the tables. A SNOW member focused on carving big blue gems the size of walnuts!

"So *this* is where the fake Hope Diamond came from," she told her father.

Mr. Spinner crinkled his nose, looking confused.

"Someone stole the Hope Diamond from the Smithsonian National Museum of Natural History in Washington, DC," she explained. "They never got caught because they replaced it with a fake like these."

"No. It's not that," said her father.

He was squinting far into the distance. She turned to see what her father was looking at and . . .

Something skittered across the floor and rolled to a stop at Samantha's feet. She picked it up.

It was a ring with a green emerald scorpion.

"Nipper's bug ring?" Samantha asked out loud. "How did this get here?"

She looked left and right. There was no sign of her brother. This was very strange.

"It's Paul!" Mr. Spinner said. "Look over there!"

Her father pointed to the opposite side of the dome, where a small alcove had been carved into the side. A glass booth stood in the alcove, close to a wall. It reminded Samantha of one of the museum cases displaying a suit of armor.

Inside the case was a figure, but it wasn't shiny and silver. It was a man wearing green plaid pajamas and bright orange flip-flops.

It *was* Uncle Paul.

Samantha took another quick look at the ring. She didn't have time to figure out how it had wound up in this place. She shoved it into one of her pockets and called to her father.

"We've got a Spinner to save," she said, hands on her hips.

Mr. Spinner looked at her, then at the statue of the brave girl.

He smiled.

"Come on," she said, pointing with her umbrella.

She led him back around the SNOW dome.

CHAPTER FIFTY-FOUR

CASE CLOSED

Samantha and her father moved from sculpture to sculpture, hurrying along the wall of the SNOW dome.

They passed the entrance, slipped behind the second lion sculpture, and kept going. Ten statues later, they reached a quartz statue of a man with one hand raised over his head. In his fist he held a long, jagged spear.

"*Zeus,*" whispered Samantha, and she smiled. "Ready to throw a lightning bolt."

A few yards away, she saw the man who had taught her all about that famous Greek statue: Paul Spinner.

Her uncle stood inside the glass case. Samantha thought he looked remarkably cheerful for someone trapped in a box.

Two SNOW agents were busy taking turns asking

him questions. Samantha couldn't hear what they were saying, but she could see the frustration on their faces.

Each time one of them asked a question, her uncle smiled and answered, and then the SNOW agents looked angrier. They banged their fists on the glass and stomped around the case several times.

Finally the two SNOW people left the case and walked off toward the center of the dome.

"This is our chance," whispered Mr. Spinner.

Samantha looked around the dome quickly. There were so many people, so many criminals. She couldn't risk letting them get their hands on the umbrella. She reached up to the statue of Zeus and pulled the lightning spear free from the god's raised hand. She set it on the floor and pressed her umbrella into his hand instead.

"You think it'll be safe there?" asked her father.

"Let's hope nobody takes a closer look at things," Samantha answered.

She stepped back to examine her work.

"If something happens to me, make sure you get the umbrella," she said grimly.

Her father nodded.

"Okay," said Samantha. "Let's crack this case."

She gestured for him to follow her, and they made their way to the case.

"Hi, Samantha. Hi, George," Uncle Paul said cheerfully, his voice muffled from inside the glass booth.

"Hello, Paul," said her father.

Samantha looked back and forth at the two men. How could they be so calm at a time like this?

"Don't worry," she said to her uncle. "We'll get you out as soon as we can."

She searched the structure for a way to open it, until her uncle tapped the glass and pointed to a nine-digit pad of glowing buttons along the back side.

"Here's hopin' the flannel can open the panel," said Samantha's father.

"Did you just make that up?" asked Uncle Paul through the glass.

Samantha's father nodded and waved at his brother. Her uncle gave him a thumbs-up back.

She ignored them both and started pressing the buttons on the side of the case. One . . . one . . . two . . . three . . . five . . . eight . . .

Beep. Click.

The buttons stopped glowing, and the door swung open.

"Fibonacci," said Samantha.

"Nice work," Uncle Paul said. "Where's your red—"

Slam!

Before her uncle could get out of the booth, a big hand reached over Samantha's shoulder and pushed the door shut again.

"Not so fast!" said a booming voice.

Samantha turned and looked up. Way up.

A new SNOW agent stood before her. His visor was red instead of green, but that's not what set him apart from the rest of the mathematicians.

He was huge!

A full foot taller than the other SNOW men and women, he wore the same white coat and the same bright white sneakers, but his sleeves were strained at the seams, and his neck was thick and bulging with muscles.

Samantha's eyes moved down to his coat pocket:

$$| X |$$

"Absolute value," said Samantha's father, reading the symbol out loud.

"Everyone just calls me *Absolute*," the SNOW man replied. "As in . . ." He switched to a high, trembling voice. "*Absolute-ly, sir. I—I'll do exactly what you tell me to do,*" he sang, imitating other members of the SNOW.

The hulking mathematician glared at Samantha and her father for a long moment. Then he looked around the dome and shouted, "Agent 33rpm! Agent 45rpm! Where did you go?"

The SNOW agents who had been questioning Uncle Paul scurried back to the alcove.

"Sorry, boss," said the faster of the two, nervously. "We needed a break."

"Yeah," said the second. "Our brains were getting mushy."

Absolute sneered at them. Then he pointed at Uncle Paul.

"Get back to work!" he bellowed. "We need to find out all that man's secrets!"

Samantha tried to look serious, but she couldn't help the smile growing on her face. They were trying to find out her uncle's secrets!

"What's so funny?" Absolute demanded.

"Nothing," said Samantha, trying not to laugh.

"Let's just slice him to pieces," one of the agents said quickly.

"Yeah," said the other. "Long division."

The two agents both smiled and held up razor-sharp rulers.

"Put those away," said Absolute. "We have to find out everything he knows."

"That's proving . . . to be . . . difficult," said one agent nervously.

"I don't care!" barked the SNOW boss. "Make him answer—and make him give us a clear, straightforward answer!"

The two underlings both sighed. They turned to face

the booth. One of them wrapped his knuckles against the glass.

Uncle Paul smiled at her and nodded.

"How are you able to travel from Seattle to the middle of nowhere?" asked the other agent.

"No place is in the middle of nowhere," Uncle Paul answered, his voice muffled from inside the booth.

"Gah!" the SNOW woman yelled, and she turned back to Absolute. "Did you just hear that? We're learning nothing."

"This man is one hundred percent mysterious," her partner whined. "And it's double-triple super-annoying!"

Samantha smiled again. She had spent four months trying to discover Uncle Paul's secrets. Every clue she'd found had always led to more questions. Getting straight answers out of him was nearly impossible, especially when you questioned him directly. If she couldn't do it, there was no way these people were going to learn her uncle's super secrets.

She fought back another laugh.

"I don't know what you think you're chuckling about," snapped Absolute. "We're *never* letting you have your uncle back."

Samantha stopped laughing. How *were* she and her father going to get Uncle Paul out of there? She listened to the sound of mine carts rolling in and out of the chamber. She heard the buzzing sound of plasma carvers and SNOW workers chipping away at blocks of salt and stone. Then she turned her back on Uncle Paul's booth and faced Absolute Value.

"You need to recalculate," she said.

The big man stared down at her, his face creased in confusion.

"He *is* my uncle," said Samantha, "but that's not why I'm here."

"So why are you here?" the enormous man demanded.

"I am a numerical overachiever, too," Samantha called loudly to everyone in the dome.

"What?" Absolute asked.

Several math agents stopped what they were doing and turned to watch Samantha. Samantha put her hands on her hips like the proud-girl statue again.

"I've come to join the SNOW!" she announced.

CHAPTER FIFTY-FIVE

CHALLENGE HER

"What?" Absolute barked, louder than before. "Is this your idea of a joke?"

He sneered down at Samantha, and she looked up at his face, trying not to peer into his nostrils.

"I'm one hundred percent serious," she answered. "I've always been a fan of addition, subtraction, multiplication . . . and imitation."

"Really?" Absolute said slowly, watching her carefully. "And *why* would *we* want you to join *us*?" he asked.

Samantha smiled and pointed over her shoulder, gesturing toward the case with Uncle Paul.

"Because," she replied, "if you let me join, I'll help you get information out of that guy."

"That guy?" blurted Absolute. "Your uncle?"

"Yes," she answered. "I can help you learn all his secrets."

Samantha was lying. She'd been trying to get answers from Uncle Paul forever, with no luck. But she wasn't going to tell that to the SNOW.

Absolute continued looking down at her. He seemed to be thinking things over.

"Hey, boss," said a SNOW agent, reaching up—way up—and tapping Absolute on the shoulder.

Samantha recognized the agent right away. It was 1+1=2, one of the SNOW agents who'd attacked her and Nipper in the museum.

"Go away," said Absolute, his gaze fixed on Samantha. "Can't you see I'm busy?"

"But, Absolute," said 2+2=4, joining her partner behind the big math boss. "That's the girl we saw in the museum carrying the red—"

Absolute turned around to face the agents.

"I said, don't bother me!" he roared.

1+1=2 and 2+2=4 quickly scurried off to another part of the dome.

"All right," said Absolute, turning back to face Samantha. "You can join us . . . if you can pass the test."

"Test?" asked Samantha.

Absolute didn't answer. He grabbed her by the shoulders so quickly that she didn't have time to react, and he steered her over to the big whiteboard in the center of the cavern.

"One, two, three, four! I declare a math war!" he bellowed.

All of the SNOW agents stopped what they were doing, and the dome went silent, except for the steady sound of mine carts rolling in and out of the chamber.

One by one, all the members of the SNOW formed a wide circle surrounding Absolute, Samantha, and the big whiteboard.

Samantha was nervous. This had been her idea, but she hadn't realized she was going to have to take a math test. Could she really outsmart a room packed with numerical overachievers? She spotted her father, standing in the circle with the SNOW. Now she was *really* glad he'd come along with her on this mission.

Mr. Spinner smiled and gave her a big thumbs-up.

"The girl's father," Absolute called to the crowd, "has wisely decided not to talk during the test."

"I have?" asked Mr. Spinner. "How did you reach that conclusion?"

Absolute pointed to a SNOW agent beside Samantha's father. She pulled a shiny, and very sharp, metal ruler out of her coat and held it up to his throat.

"You may not speak," she said to Mr. Spinner. "Understand?"

Mr. Spinner nodded silently.

Samantha gulped. She was on her own, facing whatever math test the SNOW had in store for her.

"You will now solve three problems," Absolute growled at Samantha. "Solve them and join the SNOW. Show your smarts . . . or become multiple parts."

As if on cue, several of the agents in the circle held up rulers. The sharp edges glinted in the light of the dome.

"Agent 98.6," said Absolute, without taking his eyes off Samantha. "Start us off."

A SNOW woman stepped from the ring and went

to the board. She picked up a marker, scribbled something on the board, and then returned to her place in the circle.

Samantha looked at the whiteboard:

$$1 + 2 =$$

"You have fifteen seconds," said Absolute.

Samantha looked at the board again. It was too easy.

"Um . . . three?" she replied, unsure.

"Correct," said Absolute.

Samantha relaxed a bit. Maybe joining the SNOW was going to be simple.

"Agent 186,282," Absolute called.

Another SNOW woman stepped forward.

"Come on, come on," said Absolute impatiently.

The agent scurried to the board, picked up the pen, and wrote and wrote and wrote. She zipped back to her place in the circle, revealing what she'd written:

$$674 \times 35,229 \times 0 \times 7,869,132 \times 41 =$$

"You have fifty-five seconds," Absolute snarled at Samantha.

She gulped. How was she supposed to figure this out without paper and pencil? And in less than a minute?

She tried multiplying the first two numbers in her head. There were too many digits.

"You have twenty seconds," said Absolute.

Wait. She looked at the middle of the equation. It had "x 0." Anything times zero is . . .

"The answer is zero," Samantha said.

The big man stared at her. He nodded slowly.

"Six hundred seventy-four," Samantha read, "times thirty-five—"

"I know, I know," growled Absolute, cutting her off.

The SNOW boss looked around the circle and began pointing.

"You, you, you . . . and you," he said. "Get up here . . . now!"

Four SNOW agents sprang forward and scribbled furiously on the whiteboard for several minutes. As they scattered back to their places in the circle, Samantha saw that the board was completely full.

3.1415926535897932384626433832795028841971
6939937510582097494459230781640628620899
86280348253421170679821480865132823066470
9384460955058223172535940812848111745028
41027019385211055596446229489549303819644
28810975665933446128475648233786783165271
20190914564856692346034861045432664821339
3

60726024914127372458700660631558817488152
09209628292540917153643678925903600113305
30548820466521384146951941511609433057270
36575959195309218611738193261179310511185480
74462379962749567351885752724891227938183
01194912983367336244065664308602139494639
52247371907021798609437027705392171762931 7
67523846748184676694051320005681271452635
60827785771342757789609173637178721468440
90122495343014654958537105079227968925892
35420199561121290219608640344181598132962977
47713099605187072113499999983729780499510 5
97317328160963185950244594553469083026425
22308253344685035261931188171010003137838
75288658753320838142061717766914730359825 3
49042875546873115956286388235378759375195 7
78185778053217122680661300192787661119590 9
21642019897805327951780532 1 . . . =

"You have three minutes," said Absolute.

Samantha stared at the wall of digits. She had no idea what to do.

"Two minutes, thirty seconds!" an agent shouted from the circle.

She studied the big whiteboard. What could it possibly mean? She was getting nervous.

"Two minutes!" another agent called.

Samantha scratched her head. . . . And heard music?

Her father had started whistling.

"Stop, stop, stop!" shouted Absolute. "You!" the SNOW boss growled, marching up to Mr. Spinner. "You were warned not to talk."

"I wasn't talking," Mr. Spinner replied. "I was whistling."

Absolute glared at Mr. Spinner. The large man looked over at Samantha, then back to her father again.

"Okay, okay," he said. "But not too loudly. I hate that song. It's for babies."

He turned back to Samantha.

"Continue," he ordered. "You have two minutes left."

Samantha looked back at the board. She still had no idea what the numbers could possibly mean.

Her father began whistling again. The music sounded so familiar. Then it hit her! . . . It was the It's a Big Little World song!

He'd remembered!

Last year, when the family had gone to Pacific Pandemonium Amusement Park, Samantha had made her father go on the It's a Big Little World ride with her nine times in a row. They'd rolled in globe-shaped cars while people in animal costumes sang about food around the world. By the time they'd finished, they'd been really hungry, and they'd both known the It's a Big Little World theme song by heart.

Now her father was whistling that song . . . but why?

"One minute and thirty seconds," called one of the
SNOW.

"Give up?" asked Absolute gleefully.

In her head, Samantha quickly went over the lyrics
to the song:

> There are billions of people, and like it or not,
> We ride around the sun on a little blue dot.
> Don't be unhappy. There's nothing to fear.
> IT'S A BIG LITTLE WORLD, and you're
> lucky you're here!

Samantha's head bobbed a little as she sang quietly
to herself. She pictured sitting next to her father as the
performers danced and waved oversized inflatable food
at them.

> There are waffles, falafels, and chocolate fondue,
> Burritos and sushi, and Irish beef stew.

"Thirty seconds!" called a SNOW agent.

"Ticktock," said Absolute. "Your time's almost up."

Samantha smiled. She suddenly knew why her father
had whistled this song.

> There's kielbasa and yassa, pastrami on rye.
> There's goulash, masala, and blueberry . . .

"Last chance!" Agent Absolute shouted. "What's the answer?"

"Pie!" Samantha shouted back at him.

Absolute stared at her.

"Fine," he said. "Three point one four one five nine two etcetera, etcetera, etcetera, is—"

"*Pi!*" shouted everyone in the SNOW.

CHAPTER FIFTY-SIX

LEADER BOARD

"You remembered!" Samantha called to her father. "You remembered my favorite ride!"

"It's more of a musical theater show than a ride," Mr. Spinner replied.

Samantha didn't try to argue. It felt great to know that her father had paid attention to something that mattered to *her*, even though it wasn't about lightbulbs.

"Congratulations," said Absolute. "You are now a super-numerical overachiever. Welcome to the SNOW."

He pointed to the glass case with Uncle Paul in it and gestured for Samantha to go to it.

"Now let's go squeeze some answers out of that guy," he said.

"Nope," said Samantha, not budging. "Not yet."

The big man looked confused.

"You're in the SNOW now, and I'm the boss," he said. "You have to do everything I tell you to, and now I'm telling you—"

"I challenge *you* to a math contest," said Samantha.

"What?" Absolute replied. "Why would I want to do that?"

"Because *I* know where the *red umbrella* is," Samantha answered.

"We tried to tell you, boss," one of the agents called from the circle. "We saw the girl carrying the umbrella in the museum and we—"

"Be quiet!" Absolute shouted.

He turned back to Samantha.

"I've hidden the umbrella somewhere," she told him. "You'll never find it."

Absolute stared.

"But if you can solve my challenge, I'll give the umbrella to you," Samantha continued. "You'll have the Super-Secret Plans to the whole world."

"And what happens if you win?" asked Absolute.

"Then you let my uncle go," she answered.

The big SNOW boss grunted and scratched his chin. She could tell he was thinking it over.

"Fine," he said at last. "Bring it on."

"One, two, three, four! I declare a math war!" Samantha shouted.

The SNOW fell silent. They stood, frozen in the circle, eyes locked on Samantha and Absolute.

Samantha walked to the whiteboard, grabbed an eraser, and cleared it. Then she picked up a marker.

Standing on her tiptoes, she began to write a long line of numbers, letters, and symbols along the top of the whiteboard:

$$22x-39/(9.3y^2) * 67 \times 8-\sqrt{69}m \pm 33 \div 12.000007$$
$$\times 82m \geq 4n + W^{(x+5)} + 6 * 11.4587r \times (4.56389 \pm F)^3$$

"This makes no sense," said Absolute, squinting at the board.

Samantha kept writing.

$$13B^2-45.76K \sqrt{} (4.1r) \, 33n^2-(88 \times 5h) \times 43n^2-(89-40b)$$
$$+ 7 \, 6.239-8y(x) \div 4.76^{(x-3)} \, 59.55 \div 36K$$

She glanced over her shoulder at the enormous man. "Is this a joke?" he bellowed.

"I'm not done," she answered, and continued to write.

$$6J^2 + 876-3(b-1) + 91 \, 13 \times 288y(9x) + 3j \, 63g^2-(\text{base } N)$$
$$\times 62 \, 59222.84819-2y \pm 30 \, 59.02 + 3M^2$$

The SNOW started to whisper quietly to each other. Samantha looked over at her father. He was watching intently. Far in the distance, she could see Uncle Paul. He was leaning up against the wall of the glass box, watching, too.

She continued to write.

Numbers. Letters. Symbols. Numbers. Numbers. Numbers. Symbols.

"Really?" asked Absolute. "Base N?"

Samantha stopped writing.

The board was full. She took a big step back and smiled.

251.39 ÷ [800.4 X [(997]^-2 X / (0.00390]](5") - 245 + [-4(98238929.28348 + 82p - 6605 x 2980z]] - [245r 9491000898i + 892765422f +49898 x 98M *6rl] + 7620483984.948372 x 894749j / 23746200.27632468y * 44y - 52762636T*74628474j - 3

9 + x7b - 427 - 7r +.08	14 - 9s -/- 22f * 13 - .7	11 * 45h - [9 * (780.2]]	2.31 x 7b - (9- M) / 19	6 +/- 22h * 2342.0032r	9.894 x g +/- 88/5623	22 x 7b - 3 ÷ 2	12 x 7a - (x27b] + 138
187 + 17c - H ÷ .831	62 x 3b - (2b] Ω ÷ 3.1	22 x 7b - (2b] Ω ÷ 3.8	22 x 7b - (2b] Ω ÷ 3.8	22 x 7b - (2b] Ω ÷ 3.8	22 x 7b - (2b] Ω ÷ 3.8	22 x 7b - 3 ÷ 2	1.8676239 x 8F - 647r
22 x 7b - (2b] Ω ÷ 3.8	22 x 7b - (2b] Ω ÷ 3.8	458.9 * 3i + (6j - 2258)	33 x 2h - 67 c2 x 9910	2.458373 x (7 +/- 45k)	22 x 7b - (2b] Ω ÷ 3.8	278 x r - 56.908	22 x 7b - (2b] Ω ÷ 3.8
8T - 7rT * 66.93829111	(243988867.0 * 8T) - 5	22 x 86r - 5873978.2	22 x 7b - (2b] Ω ÷ 3.8	6 x 8i - [7f] * 8r -33r -8	22 x 7b - (2b] Ω ÷ 3.8	22 x 7b - 3 ÷ 2	458.9 * 3i + (6j - 2258)
22 x 7b - (2b] Ω ÷ 3.8	22 x 7b - (2b] Ω ÷ 3.8	22 x 7b - (2b] Ω ÷ 3.8	13 + 4c - 2.13236 - 15r	55565 * 98 - 3MC +/- 2	22 x 7b - (2b] Ω ÷ 3.8	478.98 - 98H x 7y	33 x 2h - 67 c2 x 9910
2.458373 x (7 +/- 45k)	5 x 8F * 65532.99 - 7M	8M +/- 67b * 89.6 x 67r	22 x 7b - (2b] Ω ÷ 3.8	22 x 7b - (2b] Ω ÷ 3.8	5647.9 - 8X"7 - 3367T	22 x 7b - 3 ÷ 2	22 x 7b - (2b] Ω ÷ 3.8
75658998 - 3MC +/- 2	22 x 7b - (2b] Ω ÷ 3.8	22 x 7b - (2b] Ω ÷ 3.8	22 x 7b - (2b] Ω ÷ 3.8	67.98004 * 45x - 678y	22 x 7b - (2b] Ω ÷ 3.8	22 x 7b - 3 ÷ 2	22 x 7b - (2b] Ω ÷ 3.8
2.8298896002 + 879M	22 x 7b - (2b] Ω ÷ 3.8	22 - 67 +88.3 x 7b - (972b] Ω ÷ 3.8	22 x 7b - (2b] Ω ÷ 3.8	92 x 7b - (2b] / 5576.4	22 x 7b - (2b] Ω ÷ 3.8	6 x 6i - 3 ÷ 5	22 x 7b - (2b] Ω ÷ 3.8
(467*4.2 - 9.10345] / 2	62 x 7b - (2b] Ω ÷ 3.3	9 - Cb - (2b] F2+4	22 x 7b - (2b] Ω ÷ 3.8	47 - 7y - (2b] Ω ÷ 3.8	22 x 7b - (2b] Ω ÷ 3.8		14.890740592 x 38 +1

43.622 - 889.367 * 55f +/- (-74 x 8b) x 389i / [6y] x 3049 + 2y x 12Ω * 48.8 x [-6 x (99 x 308.38497r]] - 298yx + 298304.872910084z -9287840663591 x 7878.9361y * 73610.849b / 4(785720981616y) * 13 +/2 - 7209363663 + 7J(2r) -653409274.5

"You have five minutes," she said.

"Hold on," said Absolute.

"Whoopsy," said Samantha. "Your five minutes just started."

All of the SNOW agents began muttering loudly. Some scratched their heads. A few took out pencils and notepads and began scribbling calculations. Every one of them seemed very confused.

"This is beyond challenging," shouted a SNOW man.

"Four minutes," said Samantha.

"Math class was never this tough!" a SNOW woman called out.

"Enough!" shouted Absolute.

The dome went silent.

"This is gobbledygook!" he bellowed. "Nobody could figure this out!"

"So," said Samantha. "Do you give up?"

"There's nothing to give up on," said the big SNOW boss. "Most of this isn't even math. Nobody could figure out what this means!"

"I know what it means," said Mr. Spinner, raising his hand.

"What?" Absolute asked, surprised. "You do?"

"Sure," he replied. "It means I—"

A SNOW agent pressed her ruler against Mr. Spinner's throat. She looked to Absolute, as if waiting for instructions.

The SNOW boss stared at Mr. Spinner. Then he looked at the board. Then he looked at Samantha.

"All right," he growled. "Show me."

Mr. Spinner didn't move. He glanced down at the sharp ruler still pressed against his throat.

"I said let him show me!" barked Absolute.

The agent let go of her ruler, and it clattered to the ground.

Samantha's father rubbed his throat a few times. Then he walked up to the board.

Samantha held out her marker.

"Brilliant," he said softly, and took it from her.

"Come on. Come on," said Absolute.

Mr. Spinner began drawing lines around Samantha's fake math equations. When he was done, he put the pen back, returned to the ring of super-numerical overachievers, and took his place in the circle.

Everyone looked at the big whiteboard:

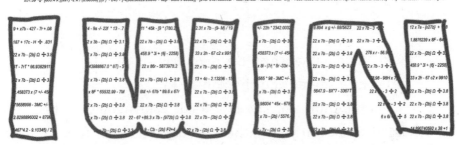

CHAPTER FIFTY-SEVEN

A GROSS GAME

"I win," said Samantha. "Let my uncle go."

Absolute smiled and shook his head.

"I don't think so," he chuckled. "He's going to be divided, and then your father will be, too . . . or four or eight."

"What?" Samantha asked. "I just gave you a challenge and you failed. Let my uncle go."

The big man nodded at her.

"That *was* impressive," he replied. "But I just wanted to see what kind of trick you'd try to pull. I'm keeping your uncle. . . . And your father, too."

"What?" Samantha cried.

"Unless you want to tell me where the red umbrella is hidden."

"No fair!" she shouted.

"I'm the boss," he snapped. "Or don't you remember? *I* get to say what's fair."

He turned and pointed at Mr. Spinner.

"Take that guy away," he called. "It's boxing time."

"I agree, one hundred percent," said Samantha's father.

Absolute's face twisted in confusion. "Huh?" he grunted. "You do?"

Suddenly Mr. Spinner turned and pointed to the entrance of the SNOW dome.

"Wow! Look over there!" he shouted. "It's a famous mathematician with an advanced degree in dynamical systems and differential equations!"

Every single member of the SNOW turned toward the entrance and stared.

"Where?" asked Absolute, peering at the tunnel. "I don't see anyone."

In one swift move, Mr. Spinner took off his hat and tossed it to Samantha.

She caught it.

"Very funny," said the SNOW boss, turning back around. "Could someone please get that girl out of my sight?"

"Sure thing, boss," said an agent close to Samantha.

But before anyone could move, Samantha held out the hat and squeezed the rim. A red boxing glove shot from the top.

Bop!

The glove struck the agent and sent her flying backward.

Absolute looked at the agent sprawled on the floor, then at Samantha.

"Never . . . mind," Absolute sighed. "I'll put them both in boxes myself."

He pushed up a sleeve, made a fist, and marched up to Samantha.

As soon as he drew near, she fired the hat again.

Bop!

It struck Absolute on the chin.

And he didn't budge.

The SNOW boss smiled down at her. Then he reached out with both massive hands and—

Samantha stepped forward and squeezed the top hat twice.

Bop-op!

"Cut that out," he said to the double punch. "Can't you see that doesn't—"

Bop-op! Bop!

The glove punched Absolute three times.

"I *said* cut that out!" he snapped. "That silly hat isn't going to—"

Boppity! Bop-op!

Samantha fired the hat at the hulking mathematician five more times. She noticed he rocked back on his heels a little after the fifth punch.

Boppity! Boppity! Bop-op!

The red boxing glove hit Absolute eight times.

"I thought I told you to stop!" he shouted.

Samantha watched him carefully. His eyes darted behind her for an instant, then locked back on to her. She spun around to see two SNOW agents charging at her. One held a pickaxe. The other had a shovel raised above his head.

Boppity! Boppity! Bop-op! Boppity! Bop-op!

Samantha blasted them with a flurry of thirteen punches. Both agents staggered backward, dropping their weapons.

She whirled back around in time to see Absolute lunging toward her.

Boppity! Boppity! Bop-op! Boppity! Bop-op! Boppity! Boppity! Bop-op!

She fired the hat twenty-one times.

Her hands were getting tired, but Absolute was starting to look worn out, too.

Boppity! Boppity! Bop-op! Boppity! Bop-op! Boppity! Boppity! Bop-op!

Boppity! Boppity! Bop-op! Boppity! Bop-op!

She sent the boxing glove crashing into the big man's face thirty-four times in a row.

"The Fibonacci sequence," a SNOW agent called out.

Absolute turned and pointed at the woman menacingly. "Be quiet!" he snarled. "I'm trying to—"

Boppity! Boppity! Bop-op! Boppity! Bop-op! Boppity! Boppity! Bop-op!

Boppity! Boppity! Bop-op! Boppity! Bop-op!

Boppity! Boppity! Bop-op! Boppity! Bop-op! Boppity! Boppity! Bop-op!

Samantha blasted Absolute on the back of his head, fifty-five times. He spun to face her but lost his footing. He stumbled and fell, landing on his rear end with a *thump*.

The SNOW boss looked up at her from where he lay on the ground. His face was as red as a leather boxing glove. Breathing heavily, he glared at Samantha. Then, slowly, he climbed to his feet. Samantha thought he might charge at her again. Instead he turned and stomped to the circle of SNOW men and women surrounding them. He walked along the ring of SNOW people and stopped beside a man holding a shiny device. Samantha recognized it as one of the carving tools that the SNOW used to cut the diamonds and crystals.

"Give me that!" he snapped, grabbing the strange tool from the SNOW agent.

He pushed a button on the side of the tool, and it began to hum and glow. Then he walked over to Samantha's father and pointed it at him.

"Hands up," he barked.

Mr. Spinner raised both hands.

"Drop the hat, girl," Absolute ordered.

Samantha froze. The glowing blue tip of the tool was inches from her father's face. Slowly she lowered the hat. Then she sighed heavily and dropped it to the floor.

"Good," said Absolute. He turned back to his prisoner. "Now you," he said. "Go stand next to the girl."

Absolute kept the device pointed at Mr. Spinner as he went to Samantha.

"You have exactly ten seconds to tell me where the umbrella is hidden," he growled.

Samantha stood, frozen, keeping an eye on the glowing machine.

"Do you think this is some kind of game?" he snarled.

He turned a knob on the handle of the menacing device. Several shapes began to blink along the body of the tool: red . . . yellow . . . blue-white.

"Tell me where the umbrella is. . . . NOW!" he barked.

Bright flecks of light sparkled and bounced. One of the glowing blue bits landed in her father's hair. It smoldered.

Samantha closed her eyes and drew a long, deep breath and held it for a moment. Then she opened her eyes and slowly let out her breath.

"Okay," she told the big man. "I hid the umbrella in the—"

"Watch out for the rain!" Mr. Spinner interrupted.

"Be quiet!" snapped Absolute.

"Ninjas, Dad?" Samantha asked. "Really?"

"No," her father replied. "I'm talking about the *rapidly approaching impact of Nipper.*"

WHAM!

CHAPTER FIFTY-EIGHT

CRASH COURSE

"Watch out for the train!" shouted Nipper.

A mine cart—with Nipper and Dennis inside it—rolled into the circle between two startled SNOW agents. Then the cart shot past Samantha and her father and slammed into Absolute. It struck him in the side, knocking him to the floor. His plasma carver flew from his hands, struck the ground, and shattered.

"Wruf!" barked Dennis as the cart kept moving past Absolute.

Samantha stood, stunned, and watched them roll past, toward the other side of the SNOW agent circle. A dozen mathematicians dove out of the way. The cart continued, careening toward the wall, directly at the case holding Uncle Paul.

CRASH!

It collided with the glass box, shattering it to bits, and came to a halt.

Uncle Paul dusted himself off and waved to Samantha and her father.

"That was a great idea, bringing the dog!" shouted Uncle Paul.

"See, Sam?" Nipper called as he hopped from the cart. "I told you Dennis would save the day."

Samantha wasn't sure exactly how the pug had saved them, or how he and Nipper had wound up in the SNOW's dome at all. But she decided she'd figure that out later, and started toward Uncle Paul.

HISSSSSS!

As she stepped over the unconscious body of Absolute, her father tapped her on the shoulder and pointed to the floor beside the man. Blue plasma seeped from the broken carving tool. It sizzled and sparked.

Samantha walked carefully around the sizzling goo and nudged Absolute with her toe, confirming he was out cold.

But beside Absolute, the plasma puddle had begun to melt into the floor.

CRACKLE!

Samantha looked more closely. Grooves were appearing in the floor beneath her feet, spreading out from the plasma puddle like a giant arachnid.

HISSSSSS-CRACK!

Samantha jumped back and watched the plasma from the broken high-energy carving tool burn into the floor of the dome. A hole formed around the device, and blue-white embers sprayed from the opening. Then the tool sank out of sight.

"We've got to get away from this," said her father, tugging at Samantha's sleeve.

CRACK!

CRACKLE!

The lines appearing beneath her feet were spreading rapidly, crisscrossing the floor like a diamond spiderweb.

The SNOW members looked frantic. SNOW men and women were turning in circles, eyeing the dome fearfully.

"The crystal lattice structure is shattering!" shouted a terrified SNOW person.

CRUNK!

At the sound, everyone froze.

CRUNK-UNK-CRUNK-CRUNK!

A huge gap appeared along the wall of the dome, then spread upward like a dreadful tree branch.

Then, *CRASH!* A hexagonal crystal the size of a car plummeted from above. It landed on a replica of an Egyptian sphinx. The sculpture shattered into a thousand pieces. Shiny fragments rained all over the SNOW.

Everyone was starting to panic and run.

Dozens of SNOW men and women dashed to the entrance tunnel. Just as many headed to the mine carts on the far side of the dome.

The umbrella! Samantha looked over at the statue of Zeus. It still stood, holding her umbrella in the air.

"Meet me at Uncle Paul," Samantha told her father. "I've to get my—"

CRUNK-UNK!

She looked up quickly. Another gap opened in the ceiling, curving overhead like a dreadful scorpion tail.

CRASH!

A huge boulder came loose and fell. It smashed a statue of a general on a horse. The granite horse's head skidded across the floor, missing Samantha by inches.

"Just go!" Samantha shouted as loudly as she could. Then she turned and dashed toward the statue of Zeus. As she ran, she spotted one of the SNOW gem makers racing between the benches, filling his coat pockets with fake diamonds.

"I'm an overachiever. But *it's-over, I'm a-leave-er!*" he said. Then he sped off for the exit tunnel.

CRASH!

Another massive boulder hit the floor. It landed next to a statue of the Egyptian god Horus. The statue fell over, shattering into dozens of topaz fragments.

She looked over at the alcove where Uncle Paul, Nipper, Dennis, and her father stood watching her.

CRASH!

A boulder fell only feet away from them and exploded into pieces.

"Hurry!" called her father.

She reached the statue, grabbed the umbrella from its grasp, and slung it over her shoulder. Then she ran.

WHAM!

The big whiteboard slammed onto the floor. It missed her by inches. She skidded to a stop, pulled her umbrella from her shoulder, and used it to point to the mine carts. They were still rolling in and out of the chamber.

"Get to those train tracks!" she called to her family.

"Watch out, Sam!" Nipper yelled back to her.

A protractor sailed past Samantha's ear and, *swack!* It snapped the umbrella off at the handle. Samantha's heart skipped a beat as the red top tumbled to the ground.

She spun around and saw two SNOW agents bearing down on her. The same agents that had been trying to get answers from Uncle Paul.

"Slow down and come with us," said Agent 33rpm.

"No, come along quickly," said Agent 45rpm.

"Get away from me!" Samantha screamed.

Still clutching the wooden handle, she searched the ground. Where was her umbrella?

RUMBLE!

A wide section of dome wall came loose. A wave of dirt and salt slid across the floor and *wham!* The salt-slide pushed over a huge statue of an octopus.

The two SNOW agents dove out of the way as the octopus statue crashed between them, crystal tentacles flying off in every direction. Samantha put the handle into her pocket. Where was her umbrella?

"Increase your velocity!" shouted her father.

Samantha looked everywhere.

"Come on, Sam!" shouted Nipper. He was standing inside a cart, holding Dennis. Her father and Uncle Paul were climbing in beside him.

"Wruf!" barked Dennis.

Samantha was frantic. She still didn't see her umbrella anywhere.

RUMBLE!

Another section of dome wall came loose. It buried a Chinese warrior statue hip deep in dirt and salt.

Samantha spun in a circle, looking for the umbrella one last time. Then she headed to the mine cart without it. As she ran, she looked back and spotted a team of four SNOW agents dragging Absolute's unconscious body toward the entrance tunnel.

"This place is crumbling!" Nipper called as she reached the cart.

"Climb in!" her father shouted. "Now!"

He helped Samantha over the side of the cart. She squeezed between him and Uncle Paul.

Her father reached for the control lever.

"Wait," said her uncle. "I see the plans."

He hopped out of the cart, raced over to a badly damaged statue of a sea captain, and picked the red umbrella up from the ground.

CRUNK-CRUNK-CRUNK-CRUNK!

A new seam opened high above them. It was enormous. Rock salt began to rain down on everyone.

"Watch out for the . . . Just hurry!" shouted Samantha.

"Catch," yelled Uncle Paul.

He tossed the red umbrella . . . but it sailed over Samantha's head.

"Got it," said her father, holding up the umbrella with one hand, his other still firmly on the mine cart's lever.

CRASH!

A refrigerator-sized block of salt plummeted onto the tracks behind them. It missed the cart by less than a foot and exploded into a hailstorm of salty pebbles.

"We've got to go, Paul!" shouted Samantha's father.

"Hurry!" Samantha called.

Uncle Paul stepped toward them, and stopped. Something had grabbed him by the collar. Behind him, the sea captain statue . . . *was moving.*

It was Nathaniel! Buffy's pirate ex-assistant!

"Aye . . . have you now!" he shouted.

"I'm not going with you," her uncle said.

"Yes you . . . arrrrr!" Nathaniel bellowed, pulling Uncle Paul away from the train.

Uncle Paul looked back at Samantha.

"Watch out for the HEAT!" he shouted.

CRASH!

Another huge block of salt smashed down in front of Samantha. A cloud of dust exploded where it had landed.

And when the cloud lifted, Uncle Paul and Nathaniel had vanished.

Samantha searched the disaster site. They weren't anywhere!

"Dad!" Samantha shouted. "Did you see that? Uncle Paul just disappeared!"

"How could I see him if he disappeared?" asked her father.

R-R-RUMBLE!

Rocks, dirt, and salt were falling all around them.

The dome was collapsing!

"Time limit exceeded," Nipper called.

Mr. Spinner pulled the lever. The mine cart lurched forward.

"No!" wailed Samantha.

"I'm sorry," said her father.

Samantha looked back, but all she could see was a swirling cloud of gray soot.

They rolled out of the SNOW dome amid a shower of salt and dirt.

R-R-R-R-OAR!

An avalanche of rock salt sealed off the tunnel behind them.

The cart sped forward on the tracks. There was no going back.

CHAPTER FIFTY-NINE

WRUF

"Largest freshwater lake?" Dr. Suzette Spinner read out loud. "That's easy. Lake Superior."

Seated on the couch in the living room, she smiled with satisfaction as she worked on the WRUF application. Most of these questions weren't difficult at all. A few were tricky, but so far, she was enjoying the challenge.

Dr. Spinner had to admit, recalling amazing facts, useless or not, was a lot of fun . . . and she was good at it. Maybe she *would* try to join that silly WRUF organization. At the very least, she'd finish the application, even if she didn't send it in. It would be good to show all the Spinner boys that they weren't the only ones capable of becoming Worldwide Reciters of Useless Facts.

It was too bad Samantha wasn't around to see Dr. Spinner filling in this form, too. Samantha would be pretty impressed that her mother also knew a lot about countries, people, and geography. Of course, Samantha would probably try to turn everything into an international mystery where her family was in some kind of danger.

Dr. Spinner scanned the page for the next question.

"Longest recorded flight of a chicken," she read out loud. "That's ridiculous. Does anyone know that? *Why* would anyone know that?"

She set the half-completed application on the coffee table.

"*Where* would you even go to find that answer?" she asked.

Then she remembered. She knew *exactly* the place to go.

Dr. Spinner left the house through the back door and headed up to the apartment over the garage. She went inside and walked straight to Paul's bookshelf.

A thin, hardcover book in the center of the top shelf caught her eye: *Poultry in Motion*.

"Leave it to Paul to own a book like that," she said.

She pulled it from the shelf and began flipping the pages. About a quarter of the way through the book, she stopped.

"Chickens," she said, reading the chapter title.

Her finger moved down the page.

"Walking . . . running . . . dancing . . . swimming . . . ," she read. "Flying."

The longest continuous flight time for a chicken was approximately thirteen seconds. That record-setting journey covered a distance of 301.5 feet.

"More than three hundred feet?" said Suzette. "Amazing. I was going to guess no more than two hundred."

Dr. Spinner nodded thoughtfully and closed the book. She began to scan the bookshelf.

"*Pirate Ships Throughout the Ages,*" she read from one spine.

"*A Handy Visitor's Guide to Llanfairpwllgwyngyllgogerychwyrndrobwllllantysiliogogogoch, Wales,*" she read off another.

Dr. Spinner grabbed both books. Then, just as she was about to leave, she spotted another book: *Major League Baseball: Rules and Special Exceptions.*

She smiled and pulled the book from the shelf.

"I'll read this one with Nipper," she said as she tucked the book under her arm with the others. "Maybe there's something in it that can help him save the New York Yankees."

Someone knocked on the door.

"Nipper?" she called. "Is that you?"

Nobody answered.

"Nipper?" she called again. "I found a book that might contain a way to keep your baseball team from getting kicked out of—"

The door burst open.

Two people in silver suits stepped into the apartment. They were dressed from head to toe in shiny foil. They wore silver boots. Their faces were hidden behind reflective metal screens. Both of them had words etched on the foreheads of their silver hoods. One said *Burns*. The other said *Swelters*.

Suzette thought the strange people looked like astronauts, or possibly scientists—the kind that explored volcanoes.

"Where's Pajama Paul?" barked Burns.

"Who are you?" asked Dr. Spinner. "What are you doing in my brother-in-law's apartment?"

"Where's the dog?" said Swelters.

Suzette sprang forward. She pushed between the intruders, bolted out the door, and stopped at the top of the staircase. In the distance, she saw several more silver figures walking around outside the house.

"Nipper! Dennis!" she called as she raced down the staircase. "Go get help! Call the police! Find Sam—"

Dr. Spinner tripped on the last step and stumbled forward onto the paved backyard driveway.

Swish!

Something dropped from above, covering her.

A net?

It was heavy. She could barely move. It was hard to see. She heard the sound of heavy boots marching down the stairs.

"We got the mom!" a voice called out. "But there's no sign of the uncle or the dog!"

Suzette was facedown on the pavement. The heavy net held her, so she couldn't get up. Shiny silver boots stomped back and forth around her.

"We'd better take the whole garage," said another voice. "Someone may be hiding somewhere inside the place."

R-r-rumble!

Dr. Spinner heard a truck or some other kind of large vehicle approaching.

"Be careful not to set anything on fire!" someone shouted. "There are a ton of papers and old books in that place!"

Through a gap between the thick ropes, she spotted a piece of chalk on the ground. She reached through the netting and grabbed it, then began scribbling on the pavement.

Hisss! Chunka-chunka-chunka!

She heard the sound of heavy machinery in the distance. Something huge was coming down the driveway. The entire backyard was shaking.

She wrote faster.

"Easy does it!" someone shouted. "You don't want to hurt anyone who might be hiding inside the apartment!"

Chunka-chunka-chunka!

Everything went black.

Vigeland Sculpture Park

In the heart of Oslo, Norway, two hundred and twelve strange and wonderful sculptures fill a public park.

They are all the work of the sculptor Gustav Vigeland, one of Norway's most famous artists. He created them between 1924 and 1943. The bronze, iron, and granite sculptures feature men, women, and children of all ages. In the statues, they are playing, fighting, and standing around in both familiar and unusual poses.

Some of the sculptures show kids wrestling, or families huddled together. The collection also includes many statues of babies standing, playing, and climbing trees. One of the sculptures features a man who appears to be fighting off a swarm of angry flying babies.

Vigeland Park also features fountains, ornate iron gates, a labyrinth, and a colossal obelisk carved to look like a tower of bodies.

Nearly two million visitors explore the park each year and marvel at the remarkable works of art.

* * *

Close to the obelisk, a huge labyrinth surrounds a fountain. The winding pathways conceal the entrance to the HEAT's super-talent training center.

Begin at the north entrance of the labyrinth and walk slowly forward along the path. Don't worry about solving the maze, however. To reveal the secrets of *this* labyrinth, you'll have to do more than take a closer look at things. You'll have to take a closer *listen!*

CHAPTER SIXTY

FASHION, DISASTER

"Mom!" Nipper called through front door of the house. "My baseball team lost."

"Hello?" Samantha called. "Why is the front door open?"

She pushed past her brother, walked into the house . . . and stopped.

The place was a mess. Books were scattered all around the living room. The coffee table was upside down, and the couch cushions had been thrown onto the floor.

"Suzette?" asked Mr. Spinner.

"Wruf!" barked Dennis as he trotted into the house.

Everyone stood looking around the room, confused.

"Wait," said Nipper, bending down to pick up some papers. "It's the WRUF application, and it's not finished."

"So?" asked Samantha.

"Maybe Mom got frustrated because she couldn't complete it," he said. "And then she wrecked the place."

"That doesn't sound like something your mother would do," said Mr. Spinner.

"Wruf! Wruf!" Dennis barked, and the light in his collar switched on and off. "Wruf! Wruf! Wruf!"

He began sniffing the couch cushions. Then he started sniffing all around the room.

"Go find what your mother's up to," Mr. Spinner said to Nipper and Samantha. "I have something important to take care of. Then I'll be right there."

He headed to his office.

"Wruf!" Dennis barked again.

"You go back outside and check in the back," Samantha told her brother.

"Wruf! Wruf!" Dennis kept barking.

"And take the dog with you," she added.

Nipper nodded and led Dennis out the front door.

"Mom! The house is a mess, and my Yankees lost!" he called, and closed the door.

Samantha walked quickly to the kitchen. It was a mess, too. All the cabinets were open. The chairs had been pulled away from the table, and one of them had been knocked to the floor.

"Mom?" she said. "Are you in here?"

The phone rang, and Samantha picked it up.

"Hello?" she said.

"Sammy!" Buffy's voice barked from the phone resting on the counter. "Where's Mother? I've been calling for hours. I need help!"

Samantha sighed. She glanced around the kitchen for any sign of her mother, while her sister continued.

"I need help," Buffy said again. "My movie is . . . Wait. What are you wearing?"

"A horizontal-striped shirt," Samantha answered.

"Well, okay. I guess it doesn't matter," said Buffy. "Nothing matters. My stars are gone!"

"Your stars?" asked Samantha. "You mean the animals in your movie, right?"

"My movie is *canceled!*" Buffy cried. "People in shiny silver suits showed up and took all the animals away!"

"Silver suits?" asked Samantha.

"Hideous!" Buffy shouted. "And my boyfriend ran away, too!"

"Your boyfriend?" asked Samantha.

"Seydou," replied Buffy. "He turned out to be a complete coward!"

Samantha heard Dennis barking loudly from the backyard.

"The moment the silver people showed up, my no-good cowardly boyfriend said he had to go to Lima."

"Lima?" asked Samantha. "Are you sure it wasn't Mali?"

"What's the difference!" her sister shouted, so loudly that Samantha had to hold the phone at arm's length. "Nobody's left! They even took the snails! And I can't stop scratching myself. . . . I have fleas!"

"As good as new," Mr. Spinner called cheerfully.

Samantha turned and saw her father standing in the doorway. He held out her red umbrella. Instead of a wooden handle, her dad had attached Nipper's hand lens to the bottom. And he'd added a self-powered lightbulb to the tip of the umbrella.

"I made some modifications," he said. "Three super-secret tools in one."

Her father twisted the magnifying glass handle. The tip began glowing brightly.

"That's nice, Dad. Very inter-esting, actually," Samantha told him. "But right now we need to find Mom."

"It was quite a light-bulb challenge," said her father. "But now it's fully operational. Here you go."

He twisted the handle again, and the light switched off. Then he held it out for Samantha. Samantha put down the phone and took the new and improved umbrella from him.

Suddenly Nipper kicked open the back door, banging it against the counter. He rushed into the kitchen waving his arms wildly. Samantha could hear Dennis, somewhere in the backyard, barking over and over again.

"It's gone!" shouted Nipper.

"What is?" asked Samantha.

"The whole thing!" he said. "The garage. The apartment. The whole thing!"

"*Earth to Spinners!*" Buffy's voice blared from the phone on the counter. "*Pay attention to me-eeeeeee!*"

Samantha and Mr. Spinner followed Nipper through the door to the backyard.

"Wruf! Wruf!" Dennis barked furiously.

The pug stood at the bottom of the staircase to Uncle Paul's apartment.

But the steps didn't lead anywhere. The apartment was gone. The whole garage had vanished.

"Wruf! Wruf! Wruf!" Dennis continued barking as he looked up the steps to nowhere.

"Don't go up those steps, old pal," warned Mr. Spinner. "It doesn't look like they connect to anything."

Samantha looked down. At her feet, five words were scrawled in chalk on the pavement:

WATCH OUT FOR THE HEAT

ALAS, NIPPER DIDN'T KNOW THESE
AMAZING FACTS!

- In 1992, the Mattel toy company came out with Teen Talk! Barbie dolls that spoke a mix of phrases when you pressed a button. One of the phrases was "Math class is tough!" Some people complained that the dolls discouraged kids from learning about math, and the company stopped selling them. Toy collectors have paid as much as $500 for them.

- Mickey Mantle was a center fielder for the New York Yankees from 1951 to 1968. He is regarded as one of the greatest switch-hitters (he could swing his bat with his left or right hand) in history. An original Mickey Mantle bobblehead can be worth as much as $1,200.

- In 1897, A.G. Spalding & Bros. introduced the No. 70 Pneumatic Head Harness. It was an early football helmet, with leather on the outside, and inflatable rubber inside. It didn't work very well, and they only sold a few of them. If you come across one, it might be worth as much as $18,000.

- Ferdinand Piatnik & Sons is an Austrian company that has been making decks of playing cards since 1824. If you find a deck from the 1800s, it could be worth $26,000 or more.

- During World War II, the U.S. Mint made pennies out of steel and zinc. They wanted to save copper, which was needed for other industries. The Mint used these other materials for one year. Then in 1944, they switched back to copper pennies, but a few steel-zinc ones were made by mistake. These few accidental pennies are some of the rarest coins, and collectors have paid up to $115,000 for one.

- The game Monopoly has been for sale since 1933. If you find one of the first sets ever sold, it might be worth as much as $146,000.

- Lou Gehrig was a first basemen for the New York Yankees from 1923 to 1939. He had so many successful seasons, he earned the nickname Iron Horse, and he was the first baseball player ever to have his number retired. One of his baseball gloves sold for $285,500.

- George Herman "Babe" Ruth Jr. played baseball from 1914 to 1935. He was the most famous New York Yankee, and one of the most famous baseball players of all time. Some people call the original Yankee Stadium the House That Ruth Built. A baseball bat signed by Babe Ruth once sold for $1,265,000!

WHOA, NELLY! THIS BOOK IS FULL OF
SUPER-SECRET SECRETS

You've probably guessed that this book is full of super secrets. So take a closer look at things and find these hidden puzzles and codes:

Journal Jumble: Just like in the earlier books in this series, there are secret hints hidden in the ID tags that appear in the top left corner of Samantha's journal entries. Copy all the letters and numbers and put them in order by section number. They'll spell out something that you might find very interesting.

The Snoddgrass Code: Everything, *everything* Missy says has a secret meaning. Once again, you can decode the numbers at the bottom of every page whenever she talks. There's one digit for each of her words. The number tells you which letter to look at in the word. For example, the number 3 and the word *that* means the letter A. If the number is 0, there's no letter for that word.

The Umbrella/Hand Lens Enigma Continues: Each chapter has umbrellas and/or hand lenses at the beginning. It turns out there's a point to them. A *point*. Get it?

Use these super-secret decoders to discover the message.

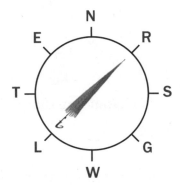

This is R, for example. (The handle is pointing to the right, and the tip is pointing to R.)

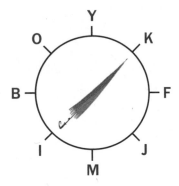

This is K. (The handle is pointing to the left, and the tip is pointing to K.)

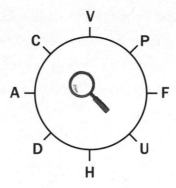

And this is *U*. (The handle is pointing to *U*.)

To learn more about all these puzzles, and a whole lot more secrets, go to samanthaspinner.com.

And if you can't get to a computer, or just want some help, keep reading!

SUPER-SECRET ANSWERS

Everyone needs a little help sometimes!
Turn the page for the answers to the
puzzles hidden in this book.

JOURNAL JUMBLE

The Puzzle:

Arrange all the entry IDs in order according to the section numbers. They will spell:

GO TO S4M4NTH4 SP1NN3R D0T C0M

4ND F1ND 4 L4DY 1N 4 H4T

CL1CK 0N TH3 H4T

Now replace all the numbers with letters:

Change every 4 to an A.
Change every 3 to an E.
Change every 1 to an I.
Change every 0 to an O.

The Answer:

The complete message is:

GO TO SAMANTHA SPINNER DOT COM
AND FIND A LADY IN A HAT
CLICK ON THE HAT

THE SNODDGRASS CODE

The Puzzle:

At the bottom of any page where Missy speaks, you will find a row of numbers. Each number signifies which letter in each of Missy's words to keep. For example, in *Samantha Spinner and the Boy in the Ball* when Missy says, "Jeremy Bernard Spinner. Stop bothering my bird. You're going to wear her out," the numbers at the bottom of the page are 6003000300000. Each digit coincides with a word Missy says. The number refers to the position of the letter in that word to use to solve the puzzle. For example, 6 means the sixth letter of the word, and 0 means no letter. Thus, the hidden word in this example is *Y-O-U*.

The Answer:

The complete message is:

GO TO MY SITE. TAP A SHELL.

THE UMBRELLA/HAND LENS ENIGMA CONTINUES

The Puzzle:

Just like in the previous books, every chapter in this book has illustrations of umbrellas and/or hand lenses. If you can decode them, you'll find that they continue the secret message that started in the first book.

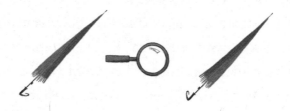

Depending on which way each one is oriented and which way the umbrella handles are pointed, each drawing secretly represents a letter. (To decode them, use the decoder wheels on pages 305 and 306.)

When you're finished, add this message to the one you found in the last book. A double-triple super-secret development in the Spinner saga will be revealed!

The Answer:

NELLY MCPEPPER AND HER TEAM HAVE ARRIVED IN THE PHILIPPINES. AS SOON AS SAMANTHA AND NIPPER REACH THE PACIFIC OCEAN, THEY WILL JOIN THEM. TOGETHER, THEY WILL TRY TO STOP THE PIRATES.

ACKNOWLEDGMENTS

This book, like the others before it, would not exist without Team Spinner.

Krista Marino, Kevin O'Connor, Kelly Schrum, and Carole Karp. Thank you!

I am also grateful to the many librarians and teachers who have been so supportive and encouraging along the way. There are too many to list, but that distinguished group certainly includes:

Mary Creek	Ray Pederson
Sue Dahlstrom	Stephanie Riddle
Jeni Freed	Charlene Saenz
Kelsey Frey	Michelle Scherbenske
Cathy Goff	Patty Smalley
Hope Harrod	Helen Tigue
Nancy Milliron	Lucinda Whitehurst . . .
Andrea Mion	

. . . and everyone, everyone at Marion Street Elementary School!

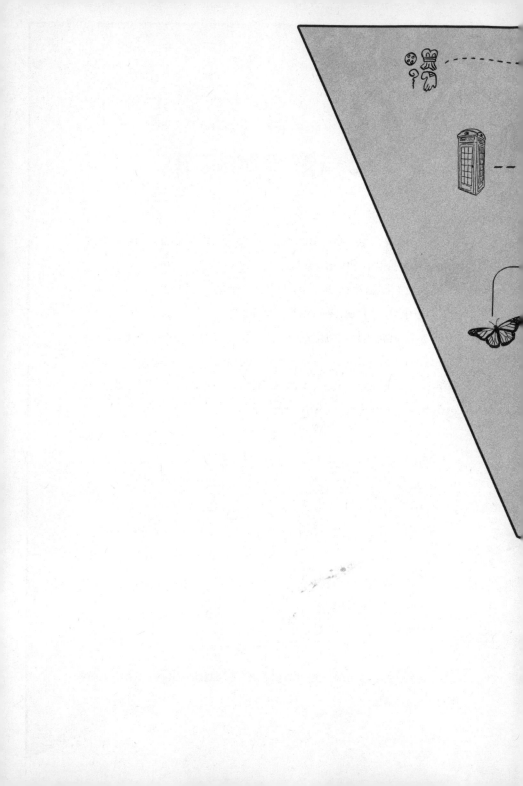

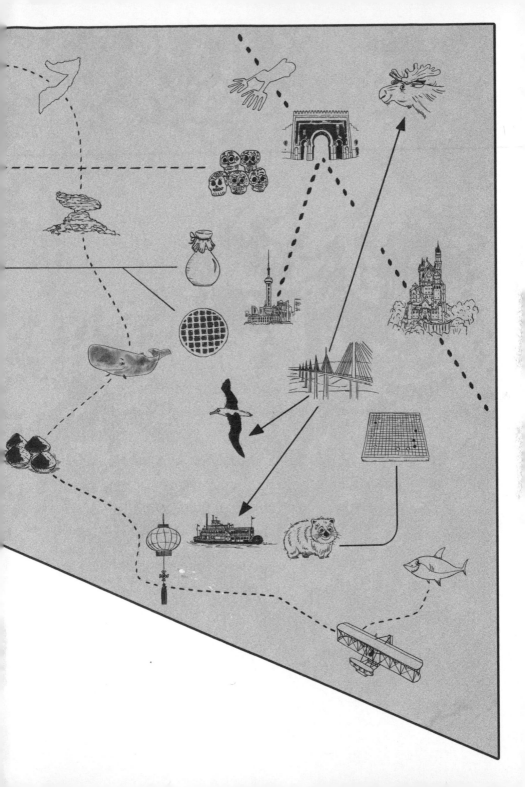

ABOUT THE AUTHOR

Russell Ginns is a writer and game designer who specializes in puzzles, songs, and smart fun. He has worked on projects for a wide variety of organizations, corporations, and publications, including Sesame Workshop, Girl Scouts of America, Nintendo, and *Scientific American*. Russell lives and writes in Washington, DC. He is the author of the Samantha Spinner series, including *Samantha Spinner and the Super-Secret Plans*, *Samantha Spinner and the Spectacular Specs*, *Samantha Spinner and the Boy in the Ball*, and *Samantha Spinner and the Perplexing Pants*. To learn more about him, visit samanthaspinner.com and follow @rginns on Twitter.